CANDLE TO THE SUN

CANDLE TO THE SUN

A collection of short stories and poems

PEGGY LEWIS

With original illustrations by William de Wilde

authorHOUSE®

AuthorHouse™
1663 Liberty Drive
Bloomington, IN 47403
www.authorhouse.com
Phone: 1-800-839-8640

First published by AuthorHouse   10/04/2011

ISBN: 978-1-4670-0107-6 (sc)
ISBN: 978-1-4670-0106-9 (hc)

Printed in the United States of America

Any people depicted in stock imagery provided by Thinkstock are models, and such images are being used for illustrative purposes only.
Certain stock imagery © Thinkstock.

This book is printed on acid-free paper.

"Knowing St George's very well from all my visits over the years and also what a wonderful place it is. I hope people will find this book interesting and it raises a lot of money for St George's Retreat".

Yours

Dame Vera Lynn D.B.E., LLD, M.Mus.

Foreword

My mother began writing whilst living in her beloved Somerset. She loved the countryside, tennis and her writers' group.

I remember the delight and, to my shame amazement, when Mum told us one of her short stories had been accepted for broadcast by the BBC Light Programme (now Radio 2) in the Morning Short Story slot. It was called *Never Go Back—and* she never did. Never looked back; never had regrets.

Mum's life was full of friends and fun except in the episodes of darkness she loathed so much in her later years. She was diagnosed with bipolar disorder in her early 60s. Her time in Buckinghamshire were the most productive in terms of writing. She belonged to the `Gillman Group', writers who inspired each other and shared the same humour and love of life.

My father died on the 12th April 1990 and my mother's mother died the next day. After such loss Mum's health deteriorated and she spent some time in a psychiatric ward. She subsequently moved to Tunbridge Wells to be near us and her adored grandchildren. She still wrote, and loved being part of a writers' group, but the very aggressive treatment she had to undergo to keep depression at bay destroyed some of her creativity but not her love of life and laughter. She regularly entertained her cherished friends from Beaconsfield as well as Bridge friends in Tunbridge Wells with wonderful food and highly amusing anecdotes. She never complained about the very powerful drugs she had to take to control the suicidal bouts of depression.

In 2006 her health took another downturn and she was diagnosed with dementia. Another overwhelmingly powerful concoction of drugs kept this, as far as possible, under control.

In the last year of her life she was looked after with immense care, love and respect by the staff at St Georges Retreat, a home run by the sisters of Augustinian Care. This home for older people with mental health problems is a model for how a good care home should be run.

Her great friend Phillip Sheahan, a member of the Gillman Group, wrote after her death in 2009

How shall we remember you?
Through the memory of laughter
The intimacy of stories shared
A smile recalled with love
A photograph never fading

With love for a bright star . . .

Janet Thornley

The proceeds from this collection of short stories, reminiscences, poems and radio broadcasts are to help further the excellent work of the sisters of Augustinian Care.

To Sarah and Martha and their children
Jacob, Grace, Ralph and Eva

With thanks to Val Wild for her intelligent suggestions, proof reading, and continuous encouragement and support.

Contents

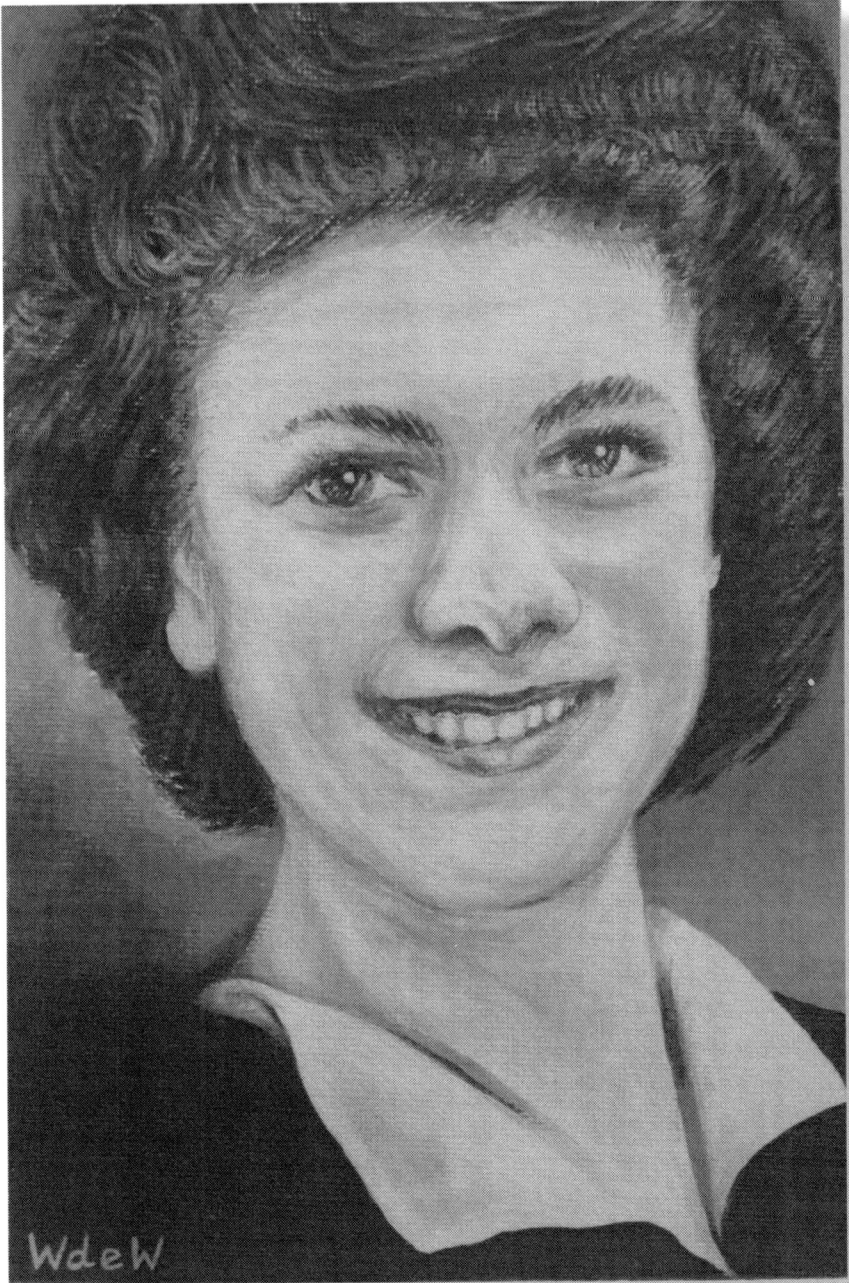

The Farewell

Six weeks after our wartime marriage, my husband was ordered to the Far East.

At the first farewell, I embarrassed him with my tears. Three weeks later, he was back on embarkation leave from Southampton.

At the second farewell, I still sobbed, but not so copiously. Three weeks later, he was back on embarkation leave from Southampton!

At the third farewell, I waved a light-hearted goodbye as the train drew out of the station. "See you in three weeks!" I shouted.

Two days later, he sailed for Burma!!

I was to learn eventually that, although the boat was packed to capacity, the passenger list was comprised of about two hundred nursing sisters, as well as the British army—which epresented about three nurses to every officer!

First Acceptance

My writing course tutor in Somerset had persuaded me to send a story to the BBC.

Several weeks later, I received a reply.

"Would you like to come and see me at Whiteladies Road in Bristol when we can discuss your story further."

My tutor was ecstatic. Framed in the doorway of the village hall with various members of the class around her, they gave me a heart rending chorus from Oklahoma to get me on my way in my old Ford through the quiet valley of the Mendip Hills to Bristol. This was 1958.

I was so nervous that the teacup handed to me by the secretary rattled in its saucer.

"Don't worry," she said. "You'll like him."

And like him I did. Snow white hair; blue-blue eyes. Incredibly kind.

He picked up my manuscript from his desk. I stared at it.

"If you're thinking it looks grubby," he smiled, "it's been well handled. Now," suddenly he didn't look so kind, "let's discuss terms."

"TERMS!" If he'd offered me half a crown I would have accepted.

"We don't pay much," he was saying, "but it IS rather an honour."

I nodded vigorously.

"And we do try to encourage young authors."

I decided not to reveal the fact that I was thirty five with a ten year old daughter. I had very rosy cheeks in those days, heightened I suppose by my tennis activities.

I peeped at him. He was so like my grandfather. I wondered if it would help my career if I sat on his lap and played with his watch chain.

As I was leaving he said, "My secretary will give you a contract."

I swallowed. CONTRACT!

Mr Coysh is still talking.

"I have to tell you that I am allowed to take TWO stories out of four hundred per month for my region. I don't know if that discourages you."

"Yes and no really," I said.

"No more purple heather or scarlet sunsets," he murmured, "Don't tell 'em. Make 'em work!"

Although I had eight stories accepted by the BBC in different regions, I never forgot Bill Coysh. I think of his voice,

"Let the listeners do the thinking. Make 'em work!"

Orchids for Mr Spendlebury

Thursday 24th July 1958
Morning short story
BBC light program

"Prudence has been kissing Mr Spendlebury in the greenhouse!" Mrs Roberts paused dramatically, and resisted the impulse to plunge her head over the top of her husband's newspaper and shout 'Yah'. The paper didn't move and she tried again.

"George! Prudence has been kissing Charles Spendlebury!"

The paper descended just sufficiently to allow a face to appear above it. It was very nice looking in a blue-eyed, crinkly sort of way–but it was a face which bore, at that moment, a resigned, long-suffering expression.

"So what!" it said, and vanished.

Mrs Roberts sighed and digested the headline confronting her that yet another satellite had been launched. "She deliberately coaxed him to go and look at the speckled orchids!" she said irrelevantly. The paper did a little, admiring swoon.

"Good for her!" applauded George. "She's got nerve. I'll say that for the girl!"

He looked across the sunny breakfast table at his wife. It was a fond look; an amused look. A look which he had regularly thrown at her over the twenty seven years of their marriage and which had just as regularly died a small death against the impenetrable wall of her vague and delightful personality.

"Be reasonable Susan!" he coaxed. "I've had the misfortune to father a buck-toothed, freckle-faced, bony daughter–and

5

who is going to deny me the pleasure of cheering her on when she scents her quarry?"

Susan crackled with indignation.

"Prudence is not buck-toothed! George! How can you say that? Her teeth are so lovely and white, that I'm sure no-one notices they protrude just the tiniest bit!"

She spread marmalade on her toast and her gentle mouth curved into a smile.

"She's not so good looking as I was, of course, but she has–well–she has . . . "

"Guts?" supplied her husband helpfully.

He rose, and kissed the top of her smooth, shining hair. She was frowning and drumming her fingers on the table, her pleasant, unlined face cupped in one hand.

"I know I exaggerated the teeth!" he murmured contritely, "but I meant the bit about the guts. She'll go far you know!"

"Yes–but she's been hugging and kissing Mr Spendlebury in the greenhouse!" she hissed at his retreating back. "I saw them!"

He waved to her from the doorway.

"Never mind, dear. I must go now–or I'll be late for the office. By the way there might be a 'phone message from the solicitor sometime today. Ring me up if it comes through will you?"

"What's it about?" Absently, she followed him into the hall.

"Aunt Sarah's will."

George glanced at himself sideways in the Regency mirror.

"You know, Sue–I'm getting a double chin. I'm not the handsome beast who led you to the altar."

"You never were!" she retorted.

"I married you for your money!"

She straightened his tie with a practised hand.

"Do you really think you were Aunt Sarah's favourite nephew, dear? After all–she only lived at the end of the village, and for the last five years she refused to see any of us."

"Sure of it!" said George confidently. "She hadn't another soul who she wanted to leave money to. She didn't even think much of cats' homes!"

"We certainly could do with some money since you lost on the Stock Exchange."

Susan sighed and glanced round their wide, elegantly furnished hall.

"It's not just us. We have everything we want. But I would like to be able to leave Prudence well-married and secure."

George opened the front door, and sniffed deeply at the warm summer breeze.

"Not to worry, Sue old girl! Remember Aunt Sarah!"

As she stacked the dishes in the sink, Susan's mind focused heavily on her daughter. Dear, spindly, intense, romantic Prudence. That was the immediate impression you had of her. Until you discovered the hard, practical core underneath! Now she was twenty five and terribly in love, it appeared, with Mr Spendlebury, who was forty two, a bachelor, and as responsive to his loved one's moods as a puppy with its new owner! Not that he looked like a puppy of any description. Rather he resembled a sad-faced red setter. And exactly what it was about him that Prudence loved, had not yet become apparent to her puzzled mother. Susan didn't really have a grasping nature, but she was firmly against her daughter marrying a poorly paid teacher of the village school, and particularly one who was seventeen years her senior.

"I know she's not pretty, "she thought, "but Charles Spendlebury isn't any oil painting either!"

She shrugged her plump shoulders, and surveyed the hazel eyes sparkling back at her from the kitchen mirror.

"He must have something!" she told herself sternly. "Prudence isn't a half wit!"

George was in a very flippant and elated mood that evening. His appointment with the Solicitor for the next afternoon had been confirmed by 'phone, and he was full of high hopes regarding Aunt Sarah's will. His wife, however, was still cocooned in her anxiety about Prudence.

"Now promise me George, you'll give me your support to prevent her from encouraging Charles! I've forbidden her to use the greenhouse as a–as a . . . "

"An Op's room?" he suggested.

"George Roberts! Do try to be serious about this!"

He made an effort to tether his wandering paternal instincts.

"Sue, darling. Prudence is almost twenty six, and she knows it! She's got no illusions about the grass being greener the other side of the hill. She's found a man and she's sticking to him! What exactly is wrong with Spendlebury anyway?"

Susan reeled off her reasons as a child recites its tables.

"He's got an odd face! He looks delicate! And well–he just doesn't earn enough money!"

She primed her guns triumphantly for another broadside, and aimed at point blank range.

"And he's nearly forty three!"

Battered but unsinkable, George returned her fire.

"Prudence likes older men. She always has. Anyway–he's not as delicate as he looks my dear. He's got good hands, and he's a mighty useful bat in our cricket eleven. Actually I wouldn't be surprised if he had quite a reserve of strength! One of the wiry sort you know!"

He glanced across at her disapproving expression, and added gently,

"Come to bed Sue and sleep on it, and I'll talk to Prudence in the morning. She's taken two weeks holiday,because his school has broken up for the summer!"

After tea the next day, Susan was watering the roses, when she heard George drive into the garage and slam the doors. Smilingly, she watched him approach her up the pathway, but her attitude changed abruptly when she saw his face.

"Something wrong George?"

It was an unnecessary question and he didn't condescend a reply, but eased himself dejectedly onto a garden seat.

"You're home early," she ventured, "oh of course, you've been to the Solicitor's."

"Fifty pounds!" George folded his arms and addressed the tall fir trees. "Fifty pounds! The old harridan!"

Dismay clutched at Susan.

"Not Aunt Sarah!" she cried. "Oh no! It can't be!"

He turned to her with a curious look in his blue eyes.

"To my dear nephew George," he quoted again.

"Fifty pounds, to spend in whatever way he wishes!"

She sank beside him on the seat.

"But who else . . . ? I don't understand . . .!"

Slowly, George dropped his words into her mind as a man would drop pebbles, one by one, into a pond. He watched ripples of realization and horror spread across her face.

"To Mr Spendlebury," he said, "the kind friend who spent so many patient hours playing the piano to me when I was ill. The sum of six thousand pounds!"

Susan choked.

"Six–six thousand? Say it again! Oh George! Say it again!"

"Six thousand!" obliged George gloomily. "And I thought I was her favourite nephew!"

"But you were, George darling!" Susan looked at him distractedly. "There was only Percy, and he went to Australia–and she never liked him anyway!"

She started to pace up and down the path, banging the palm of her hand with a small clenched fist.

"What are we going to do? Whatever made her leave all that to Charles Spendlebury? He's so weak George! He's as spineless as a jellyfish!"

Miserably she added, "He's not even a young jellyfish!"

George dug his pipe from the depths of his jacket with the air of a man seeking the assurance of a trusted friend. He tamped the tobacco thoughtfully.

"Susan my dear. Surely your chief objection to Spendlebury was that he didn't earn enough money."

He reached across to her quickly, as she drew abreast of him in her frantic pacing and, gripping her around the waist, he plumped her beside him on the seat.

"Well–just think about it a little. Is anything else so very important in comparison with six thousand pounds?"

Susan went rigid and a deep indignant flush spread over her face. She addressed him dramatically.

"I never thought I would see your daughter sold to the highest bidder George!"

He was completely unperturbed.

"He's the only bidder my dear!" he reminded her mildly. "And I'm trying to balance six thousand pounds against a sluggish mind and two score years and three!"

"Prudence could never be happy with him," fretted Susan. "He would just pull her down to his dreary level, and they would have a gaggle of drab, colourless children!"

She paused to wallow in the pitiful picture of her daughter's married life

"I'm not so sure," George said slowly. "I'm not so sure."

He cradled his pipe in one hand, and gazed unseeingly at a rambler trailing its crimson roses from an archway over their heads. Still without looking at her, he placed a gentle arm around her until her head came to rest on his shoulder.

"I've been thinking, Susan."

His tone was measured and brooding.

"Has it occurred to you that Prudence might have had a hand in all this business?"

He sat forward suddenly, and snatched the pipe from his mouth.

"Well, I'll be damned!" He slapped his knee. "I remember now. It was last Autumn, when we heard that Aunt Sarah had orders to take things very easily because of her heart."

"You almost broke my neck, jerking forward like that!" grumbled Susan. "What was last Autumn?"

"Well I overheard Prudence and Spendlebury chatting on the verandah when I was in my study. I distinctly heard her telling him that Aunt Sarah loved listening to the piano, but that no-one had the patience to go and play to her!"

Susan looked quite overawed.

"How splendid of her to think ahead like that!"

"Splendid my foot!" snorted her husband. "Do you realize she had her plans all cut and dried nine months ago? She's a scheming little minx, and she ought to be ashamed . . . "His voice trailed away.

"Well–perhaps it was rather splendid!" he admitted. "You know, my dear, if she decides to marry Spendlebury, she'll make him a spanking good wife. And with a dynamo like her behind him–who knows how far he'll soar?"

He turned to face her and took her hands in his, holding them tightly.

"Honestly darling, I feel this makes all the difference to allowing her to–er–continue the chase, don't you?"

Reluctantly, Susan felt her prejudice slowly melting before the warmth of her admiration.

"If Prudence can organize an underground movement like that for nine months," she thought, "it will take a stronger mother than me to sabotage it!"

George was still talking.

"After all–look what she's done for him already. The man's richer by six thousand pounds!"

Surrendering to a force greater than her own, she rose and walked pensively to the edge of the lawn.

"They're sitting under the oak tree," she murmured and gave herself a little shake as though shedding the last of her burdens.

In that moment she seemed to grow in stature and, standing there, shielding her eyes from the sun, she vaguely reminded George of some great warrior queen summoning her tribes to a pagan ritual! Her voice when it came was ringing and decisive.

"Prudence?" she called. "Prudence! I'm over here by the rose garden. Er–your father and I were just wondering . . . why don't you take dear Mr Spendlebury into the greenhouse–and show him the orchids my love?"

The Snapshot

First published 14th August 1961
Evening News and Star

She had never really believed it could happen to her! Slowly, she straightened up from the desk and started staring around at her shadowing lounge, the snapshot clutched in her hand. She had planned this room when all the deep fulfillment of marriage with Joe had given her an instinctive flair for elegance and beauty. The polished leather, the flowers, the shelves of books were her own outpourings of delight in the happiness of her joyful marriage.

Her fingers curled over the tiny snapshot and crumpled it a little as she walked out to the stone terrace where the pale, evening sunshine was turning the last chrysanthemums into lacquered gold. She paused suddenly, hardly knowing why, to stare up at the tall Regency house where she had lived for so many treasured years. Her mind drifted back slowly to the deep twilight of an early year of war . . .

Newly-married, she had stood with Joe in the quiet square, and they had been silent together and very happy, to know the house was theirs. There was a great warmth about Joe. In their first few months together, she knew ecstasy and splendid peace. She took joy in their unborn child.

When Joe had been called up, he hadn't been sentimental or dramatic. That wasn't Joe! On the last day of his embarkation leave, there was a stillness about him and a strength, which carried her through the labouring years of war until young Robert had started at nursery school, and Joe wrote to say he was being demobbed and would soon be home from Italy for good. It had been a long hot August day, and the high glass dome of the station was touched gently with pink and saffron as she met Joe on the crowded platform. The suppressions and futility of separation became miserable uncertainty at not being able to tell this tall stranger how much she had missed him and longed for him over the lonely years.

The time had passed quickly and their second son, David, was born.

"Don't you want a daughter sometime, Joe?" she had asked.

He had been silent and she saw a depth of worry in his eyes. Then he spoke awkwardly, as though explaining something to himself rather than to her.

"It's a question of expense. Things are going to be pretty tight for a while I'm afraid, and I want to send the boys to the best school I can afford—"

She had smiled at him.

"Don't worry. Don't think about it any more. If that's the way you want it, I understand."

But she hadn't understood at all . . .

Now, she paced in the garden looking up at the house and shivering in the frosty air. Slowly, she became aware of the crumpled object in her hand. She walked into her immaculate kitchen and switched on the light, to stare again at the snapshot. She barely glanced at the lovely, dark-haired woman and the tall, brown-skinned boy at her side. Instead, in cold misery, she read once more the inscription written carefully on the back. It was brief, and terrifyingly intimate.

"To Joe, from Maria and your dearest son, Pietro."

Pinned to the corner was a slip of paper on which someone had printed "On holiday in Florence." When she had found it in the desk with some documents which Joe had filed away, she guessed there had also been a letter and that Joe thought the snapshot was still in the envelope.

She wondered what he would say when she showed it to him. She would have to tell him she had found it, of course. When you had lived with a man for fifteen years—and he was your husband, lover, companion and consoler—you couldn't think of keeping something like this locked away in shameful darkness. Neither could you think of flaunting it before him with hurt pride and wet eyes! All you could do was to stand there, as she was doing now—numb in your unhappiness—remembering only the pleasant things and the warm things about your life together.

She heard Joe's key turning in the lock. Deliberately she walked into the hall, and stood for a moment watching him. You'll never know, she thought, the happiness you've brought to me, because no words of mine could ever tell you. I have only been able to show you in a thousand stupid ways, which perhaps you have never noticed.

Her voice was tense and thin.

"I found this snapshot in your desk this afternoon!"

His dark eyes were expressionless as he looked down at it, and she wondered why everything around them in the hall seemed suddenly watchful and still. His voice, at last, was very gentle.

"I'm sorry you had to find it, Elizabeth. I wish I could say more than that. I'm sorry."

She followed him into the rose-curtained lounge, and silentl he handed her a cigarette. Bending to light it for her, he asked,

"Where are the boys?"

She felt slightly hysterical. How could he ask an ordinary question like that?

"Over at the Hewisons. They said they'd be back for supper."

She sank onto the settee and held out the snapshot to him almost appealingly.

"If this happened when you were in Italy, why couldn't you have told me before? Why did I have to find out like this?"

"I didn't mean you to find out at all!' said Joe simply. He sat on the arm of a chair and looked straight at her with a strangeness in his eyes.

"I felt it better you shouldn't know. You've been fairly happy, haven't you—over the years?"

Fairly happy!! His words choked her.

Reluctantly, he stubbed out his cigarette. There was an expression on his face as he looked across at her which she was too upset to recognize as pity.

"I met Maria in Salerno." He saw the woman's name stab her, and he said quietly,

"I'm sorry, Elizabeth, but it wasn't just a brief passing affair. I loved her very much. She was beautiful, warm and affectionate and I saw her whenever I could."

Hatred rose suddenly within her.

"A woman of no account!"

"No!" Joe's voice was curt.

In terrifying loneliness she whispered, "Pietro! Your son!"

Joe answered with unconscious pride.

"He'll be twelve this year."

Desperately she thought: 'Now I shall never know how you have longed for her over the years.'

"Why didn't you stay over there with her, Joe? Why did you come back to me?"

"It's all over now!' he said abruptly. "Except for the boy!"

Falteringly she asked,

"What do you mean—except for the boy?"

Joe's voice was steady.

"I want him to be educated in England with Robert and David . . . I've been trying to save towards it every year!"

This time, she recognized the quiet pity in his eyes as he came to her across the room and she knew, as surely as she knew anything, that she must not plead with him or tell him how hurt she was.

"You must think about it, Elizabeth. You've got every right to be angry and every right to leave me, if that's what you want to do!" He looked down at her anxiously. "I'm saying this at the wrong moment, but I have always loved you."

"In your fashion!"

She regretted her words instantly. But he merely put his hands in his pockets, and turned away from her. She could only see the broad outline of his shoulders. And his voice, when it came, was drained and emotionless.

"I want Pietro to come over here soon . . . because Maria died last week."

Elizabeth gasped, and stared at him incredulously, as Joe went on.

"The snapshot was from her brother. She was going to send it to me and he thought I'd like it."

For a long moment, she stayed there with him, struggling to speak. Everything had changed, and yet nothing had changed. This was still Joe, standing there with his back to her in his dark, city suit. She noticed, ridiculously, that it was getting a little shiny at the elbows.

Robert and David would be on their way home, and through the window she could see a pale petal of moon poised on the edge of a chimney pot.

Silently, she turned and left the quiet room, closing the door behind her, although she knew instinctively that Joe would not attempt to follow her. She walked across her soft bedroom carpet to the window overlooking the bending trees. In the darkening garden the last leaves were marching and swooping under the naked arms of the branches like children playing an endless game of oranges and lemons, and she leaned her head against the window, closing her eyes and fighting back the tears. Sometimes, she thought, you can ache with a longing for comfort; there is a sweetness about it, and a sadness, and an unnamed fear. But she knew only that she had wanted everything to stay as it had been yesterday. And that nothing would ever be the same again . . .

But Never To Us

First published 4th February 1963
Evening News and Star

She had never quite recovered from the early rapture of her marriage. There had been an easy familiarity about those seven years, and a certainty and completeness in their being together that dissolved all the crowding problems of each new day. There had been the usual spate of quarrels and grievances. Small ones. But this quarrel was different! For the first time since she had lived with Pete, Maggy faced the morning with a mind as dull and heavy as a winter smog. She heard Pete leave the bathroom. Usually, he ruffled her dark hair, but this morning his eyes looked past her in the mirror as he whipped on his tie, and he merely said:

"Better buck up. I'm not too early."

Without a word, she went downstairs to her shining kitchen. Through the window she saw the early morning sun gilding the branches of the garden trees, and down in the orchard the daffodils she had planted raised their bright heads to the sky. Everything is the same, and yet nothing is the same, she thought. Yesterday, Pete and I were happily married. We had our house and our child and each other. Nothing seemed so important that it couldn't wait until tomorrow. And now . . . She fought back her tears, remembering their quarrel last night, which had been of her own making.

She had been frightened and miserable since her discovery that afternoon when she had opened the wardrobe door. The sports jacket was the first thing she looked at. Pete wore it round the house and garden every weekend, and it begged to be cleaned. She started to turn out the pockets. It was then she found the letter. Seeing that the handwriting was Pete's, she had thought it was some office notes that he had forgotten to transfer to his city suit. In that swift, appalling moment the chrysalis she had built around her exploded in a burst of fear!

"My Darling,

I don't think I can manage the weekend after all. It looks as though it will have to be the following Saturday. It seems so long since I was last with you, and I can hardly wait until our next meeting.

The time will soon go by, and when I see you, I'll be able to tell you again how much I love you. Look after yourself, my dearest. You are always in my thoughts.

Your loving Pete"

There was no address and no date.

With a dreary little gesture, she had pushed it back in the coat pocket, and returned the garment to the wardrobe. She didn't know how long she had stood there, numb in her unhappiness remembering, at first, only the pleasant things about their life together. Remembering, too, another Pete; the one whose glance would linger on a pair of pretty legs, and whose dark eyes could charm the birds off the trees. She visualised him handing the note to some woman at the office, perhaps. Possibly even now he was hunting for it in the pockets of his city suit, wondering where he had left it. Slowly as she closed the wardrobe door, she knew she must find the courage to speak to him that night. The poison in her mind channelled into vindictive sharpness, and her temper brought a growing stubbornness to Pete's mouth.

"What's wrong, Maggy?' His voice had been calm, and strangely gentle.

She had almost asked him then, about the letter.

His hand was on her shoulder, and in her worry and confusion, she had knocked it away.

"Leave me alone, Pete, will you?"

His anger had mounted then . . .

And now, after the quarrel, it was morning and breakfast time, and soon, the bright sunflower head of her daughter would be bobbing over Pete's shoulder as she rode on his shoulders down the stairs. When he appeared in the doorway, she knew by the way his eyes sought hers that he was half way to forgetting the night before. Bitterly, she thought, perhaps you know another woman as well as you know me, and I shall never discover how often you think of her, or need her. Or whether you need me still!

"Young Jane was asleep," he said. "I didn't disturb her."

Then he kissed her, and she was left to wonder how a golden day could seem so drab and cheerless.

All through the long morning she worried and reasoned, while Jane's burbling laughter echoed round the house. She thought of the people she had known in the seven years she had been married to Pete. Some of their marriages had crumbled, and she remembered how shocked she had been when one of her closest friends had left her husband for another man. Pete had said:

"I know, Maggy, I know. We feel it could never happen to us, but it happens every day, darling. And when you least expect it!"

When you least expect it!! At six o'clock, she heard the crunch of footsteps on the gravelled path. He was smiling as he put his arms around her.

"Came home early to fit some gardening in after dinner," he was saying. "I'll go and change now."

She felt a throbbing, physical ache, because recently some other woman might have been waiting for him as she was waiting now. After the meal, he slipped on his old jacket, and she trembled so much when she saw him wearing it, that he insisted on making the coffee and carrying it out to the stone terrace.

"You must have caught a chill," he said, "shivering like that just now."

I shall ask him this minute, she thought. He's wearing the jacket, and I shall ask him . . . Pete suddenly put down his coffee cup, and delved for his pipe and tobacco. She wondered if he could hear the beating of her heart, as the letter appeared in his hand. In that one revealing moment, he had glanced at it, and tried to push it back. Almost calmly she had studied his face before he looked across sharply and saw her watching him. Laughter glided instantly over the guilt. Instant laughter. Instant charm.

"Meant to tell you about this," he said, tapping the letter. "You'll never guess where I found it the other day! At the bottom of my sock draw!"

She stared at him.

"Shows how often you sort out my socks!" he grumbled. "You don't deserve to be thought about as much as I thought about you when I wrote this! Still I grant you, it was right at the back of the drawer!"

She was still staring at him, her lips parted and her fingers curled tight around her cup.

"Do you remember," Pete was saying, "when I was sent on that course at Ashford, and we had only been married six months?"

"Yes. Yes, of course I do."

"I wrote this letter when I thought I couldn't get away one weekend. But I managed to wangle it after all, so I never posted the thing! Lord knows why I kept it, but I found it yesterday tucked inside an old map I had with me on the course!"

In the distance, Maggy heard the laughter of her daughter as she played with a small friend in the garden, and her eyes ached for the relief of tears.

"Shall I read it?" Pete asked.

"Go right ahead," she said, looking away from him. "It might give me the energy to wash up!"

She turned slowly to see Pete's dark head bent over the letter, and she felt the burden of a wisdom that was also a release. Fiercely she thought: I'll hold you because I need you! And one day, you'll need me too! I'm a fool, and you're a liar. A fascinating liar! . . . But I shall never let you know.

Now is Now

On a dog-day afternoon, I found where father's father lay.
Parchment corn streamed to pearl horizons.
A painter's light anointed Flatford Mill.

Father's father. Agronomous. With prim fingers.
Contentment was thankfulness for daily bread.
Grief was buried
In a Flanders' field, with fledgling sons beneath the poppies.

On either side of father's father slept
Liza Jane and Thomas John.
His friends in life; companions, now, in death.

A wastrel rose hugged all three tombstones in its thorned
embrace
Snowing its petals on the summer grass. With the same
Intransience of cupping water in the palm before its
draining,
I recalled our walks when land was lazy, and the milk-mist
dawns
Shrouded the day's fragility.

Thistledown world. Morning world.
Before reality played handstands with my dreams. Before
I knew
That flowering ends with dying. Before I watched a love
Turn sour in two most close to me.

Fretful, I'd stood
With square-cut fringe and tongues of hair licking each
cheek,

White-collared and gingham-dressed.
My polished shoes had rubbed
Upon my ankle-socks a darkened ring, as father's father
spoke.

'They've gone their separate ways, child. No-one's fault.
Some must have their freedom, while others are diminished
by it.'
Despairing, I claimed my bonds of flesh. He looked away.
'Possession isn't love. Now is now, and we mustn't think of
maybe.'

In evening light, he fed me buttered scones, and lettuce
leaves
Like crisp and crinkled tissue.
And sugared raspberries in china bowl.
The wall-clock nagged, with flat, reproving chimes as if it knew
My mother waited, empty, needing me as solitary proof of
consummation
In her traumatic coupling.

My father's father beckoned from the hall,
His sapless, ivory hand blue-branched with veins.
Neat-flagged his path, a perforation to the gate.
He'd pause to join an errant shoot to parent stem. Or to
appraise
A silver moon. A basic man, his joys in basic things.

I touched the tombstone, skewed with age. My ghosts were
silent.
'Freedom is all,' he'd said, this Suffolk son,
Asleep down there, where the briar roots are strong,
His water-colour skies above his head.

Interlude

First published 12th December 1964
Woman's Own

She walked, as always, like a queen—tall and lovely with a careless grace. The man, watching her as she crossed the hotel lobby, hurried to meet her and took her hands in his, admiring her.

"You're as lovely as ever, Elizabeth!"

She laughed.

"It was good of you to phone. It's been far too long."

"Eight years? It must be that, at least."

Again she laughed, flicking her dark hair away from her face, her eyes warmly responsive.

"How's Simon?"

He was deliberately casual as he steered her to the softly lit dining room.

"He's very well, and sorry he couldn't get here tonight. He's been so busy lately at the office that I'm often in bed when he comes home."

She was peeling off her black gloves and looking round at the other tables with such interest on her lively face that he felt the years falling away. 'She was pretty before,' he thought, 'but now she's beautiful.' He ordered the meal and wines with the assurance of a man who dined out more frequently than he dined at home.

She said solemnly, "You're looking older Peter, and it suits you!"

"I ripened slowly," he said. "The best fruit always does!"

She chuckled, and propped her chin on her hands.

"I know you have at least one child. And are you happy?"

His dark eyes were watchful.

"Two children. Boys. Yes, indeed I am happy."

Her eyes widened but she said nothing.

"May I ask you the same question, Elizabeth? Did you find happiness?"

"Yes!" she said fiercely—too fiercely. "I have a daughter, and she's seven. I love her very much!"

"And Simon?"

"He's a wonderful husband. He's very kind to me."

He was silent and his face was expressionless, but she knew he was waiting for her to say: 'I love him!'

Instead, she said again:

"He's very kind!"

She avoided his gaze and turned gratefully towards the waiter, as he approached them with a laden tray.

Later, they danced, and then Peter drove her home along the road winding by the river. When they reached her house, she asked him in for a drink; Simon was there, yawning over the meal she had left him in the elegant room. She watched their evident pleasure at meeting again and then asked:

"Have you just come home, Simon?"

He nodded as he poured out drinks.

"'Fraid so, darling! And it looks as though I'll be late for quite a while!"

"Oh, no!"

Elizabeth stared at him, dismayed in her concern, forgetting Peter.

"It isn't good enough, Simon!"

He gave her a warning glance as he walked across the room with the tray, but she didn't heed him.

"No one else does it. Why should you be the first one there and the last one home? You might just as well not have a daughter, she sees so little of you!"

She knew she was saying too much and she was almost relieved when Simon reached for a box of cigars, and she heard his muttered:

"Pack it up, Elizabeth! I know you're probably tired, but we've got a guest."

25

As far as Simon was concerned, if a woman argued, she was tired or depressed; and it was perilously near to nagging. If a man argued, he was guided by solid good sense, resulting in discussion and solution! Peter was watching her, and his dark eyes held compassion as well as laughter.

Next morning, she walked slowly downstairs to her kitchen and swished back the yellow rose-patterned curtains. Then she made the coffee and lit the grill. 'Everything is the same, and yet nothing is the same,' she thought. 'Yesterday, Simon and I were happily married. We had our house and our child and each other. Nothing seemed so important that it couldn't wait until tomorrow.'

Her heart contracted suddenly and she put down the coffee-pot and fought back her tears, remembering her determination to make her marriage a success, because she had always known that she was not in love with Simon. From the moment of meeting Peter again, she had felt only restlessness and a strange, deep longing which almost frightened her. She had hoped that eight years without seeing him would have made her forget how hurt she had been when he had married Harriet Townley and sailed to Johannesburg within the month. She had still been under the spell of his quiet yet utterly demanding personality when she rebounded into a marriage with one of his closest friends—a man called Simon!

Now she wished with all her heart that Peter had not phoned her on his brief business trip to England. If only Simon had been able to come too, she might have found it easier to resist the compulsive attraction that made her ache with longing. When the telephone rang mid-morning, she answered it almost fearfully.

"How are you, Elizabeth? Thank you for making my evening so enjoyable yesterday."

"You're thanking me?"

"Of course. The horrible alternative would have been dining with a business acquaintance, or my Aunt Jenny from Wallington!"

"You're so complimentary!"

She was smiling now, wondering why she had been apprehensive. He paused.

"You know I told you the firm may be moving me to England? Well, it could be pretty soon, according to London office. So I'm thinking of searching for a house." Abruptly he added: "Can I see you again soon?"

She laughed. "What's that got to do with looking for a house?"

"Nothing at all!" he confessed. "But from now on, I can use it as an excuse for needing your company! Shall I call for you at twelve-thirty?"

"No!" she said hastily, picturing the relish and speed with which certain neighbours would inform Simon of her visitor before she could tell him herself. "I'll meet you at the Crown in the HIgh Street in half an hour."

Slowly, she replaced the receiver, planning her day calmly and without emotion. She would be home before Lucy came in from school at four-thirty, so as soon as she had made the beds, she could get ready to go. She felt strangely disturbed and elated as she changed into her new winter suit. Elizabeth was not aware that she was on the threshold of being unfaithful to Simon, because she was not even trying yet, to compare her husband with Peter. She knew only that she felt young and vital, while the shining day was full of promise.

After lunch at the Crown, they drove to see some country houses the details of which Peter had obtained from an agent. Elizabeth became happier with every minute of the swiftly passing day. Her happiness persisted long after Peter had driven her home, so that Lucy became wildly infected by her gaiety and was singing to herself upstairs in bed, as Simon's key turned in the lock.

"Darling!' said Elizabeth, surprised. "I thought you were working late tonight!"

"Too tired!" he said. "I've had a hell of a day!"

"Sit down, Simon. I'll pour you a drink. How long have you got to work like this, for heaven's sake?"

He downed his drink with a gulp, and silently held out the glass again.

"Until I've got the new department really swinging! Shouldn't be too long now! To you, darling!"

This time, he raised his glass to her. "What's your day been like?"

"Oh, typical!" she said evasively. "Except that I've been out with Peter this afternoon."

He looked at her. "You have?"

"To see some houses with him," she explained hastily. "His firm may be moving back to England soon, and he phoned me to ask my advice."

"Good idea!" Simon stood up and stretched. "I expect he is going to have a pretty busy leave, fitting in all his old friends."

Like a pebble in a pond, her first deception was hardly noticeable.

"Yes," she said carelessly. "I don't suppose we"ll be seeing much of him!"

But she knew, as surely as she knew anything, that Peter would phone her again.

Elizabeth could never quite pinpoint when she decided not to tell Simon about her second meeting. Then she found it impossible to mention all the other times. Two weeks later, she drove with Peter to a lake near the sprawling sleepy town, and her mood was one of elation mixed with sadness, anticipation mixed with fear. Peter was quiet as they walked beside the lake, and she herself felt uneasy and troubled. Hands in pockets, he scowled into the sun.

"What are we going to do?"

She didn't pretend to misunderstand him. Miserably, she said: "I don't know! I just don't know!" And then she burst out: "Why did you marry Harriet?"

He shrugged. "Perhaps it was because her father had money!"

"I don't believe you!" she said furiously. "Besides, it was me you loved!"

"Oh, no it wasn't!"

He stopped to stare at her, a strange expression in his dark eyes.

"If that's a bubble you have preserved all these years, Elizabeth, I hate to prick it but I certainly didn't love you more than Harriet! You were too immature! Lovely, but immature!"

Slowly, then—slowly and gently—so that her nerves were screaming for his kiss before it came, he took her in his arms and placed his mouth on hers, turning the golden day into ecstasy, as yielding as velvet and honey-sweet. He looked down at her, still holding her.

"You've changed more than I would have thought possible," he said wonderingly. "I suppose marriage has done this for you. You were completely unawakened when I went away."

She moved restlessly in the circle of his arms.

"I wasn't aware I had changed at all."

She was still trembling from his kiss. There was no feeling of guilt, only a blinding knowledge of forces beyond her control and a certainty that she needed no other man. His arms tightened around her again, and she wondered if he knew the power he had over her.

"There used to be an inn," he was saying thoughtfully, "called the Fox and Hounds, I think. Near the coast. Can you manage a week-end with me, Elizabeth?"

Without any hesitation, because her emotion was still swamping her, she heard herself saying:

"Simon has to go to Manchester on Friday for five days. I could send Lucy to my sister for the weekend. She's been asking for ages . . . "

She faltered a little then, and Peter was gentle.

"Are you sure, my darling?"

"I'm sure!"

While he was with her, she had no doubts, no fears. His presence made her forget that she belonged to anyone else, and she was no longer a wife and mother, but someone who was magically in love.

Two days later, in the hall, Simon kissed her goodbye, and turned to pick up his case.

29

"Give my love to Lucy. Tell her I might bring her a present from Manchester if she's a good girl while I'm away."

'Now,' she thought, 'now you must take me in your arms and plead with me, please, Simon! Tell me you need me. Tell me you love me. Please, Simon!' But he simply touched her cheek with his fingers.

"Goodbye again," he said, and she wondered for a moment if she had imagined the uncertainty in his voice.

She was still remote and a little unapproachable when she met Peter. He was wise with women, and he understood them surprisingly well so he merely took her case and drove her in silence towards the open countryside. After a while, he looked sideways at her.

"Lucy off with your sister and Simon in Manchester?"

She nodded.

He reached out and laid his hand on hers for a brief moment, his eyes intent, now, on the wide, busy motorway. "Don't worry," he said.

The inn was quaint, with mullioned windows and mauve wisteria. But there it ended. Inside, the paint was peeling, and an air of decadence etched every room. The evening meal was mediocre, and Peter became more and more restless, as a mournful waiter served them with lukewarm coffee in a brown and beige lounge.

"I wish we'd gone on somewhere else before we booked in. It certainly wasn't like this years ago."

"There's nothing for at least thirty miles," she said wearily. "You know there isn't!"

His eyes searched her face, and he found it troubled and a little afraid. Abruptly, he said:

"Let's see what the bedroom's like. It can't be worse than this!"

But it was. Infinitely cramped and depressing, with a bed that was concave in the middle. Suddenly, she wanted to laugh. 'This,' she thought, 'is where the man feels ridiculous and if I laugh at him, he'll hate me.' But Peter didn't look at all ridiculous as he closed the door and leaned against it, looking at her thoughtfully.

"I decided not to go through with this about four hours ago!" he remarked casually.

Her desire to laugh receded.

"I just don't believe you," she said weakly. "I told you I'd come away for the weekend and I meant it."

"At the time!" he finished. "But I wish you could have seen your face when I met you this evening. You looked as though you were beginning a stretch in Holloway!"

"Peter, I'm sorry."

"So am I, because I love you, and I needed you, and I think we would have been very happy."

At his words, emotion and desire began to rise in her again, and Peter, watching her, knew he still had the power to play with her feelings like a conjuror with a pack of cards.

"Come on!" he said suddenly. "I'll drive you home."

"No, Peter! I promised."

"I'm not being noble," he said roughly. "I just know enough about women to realise that for one weekend with me, you would suffer a lifetime of regret! You're just made that way! Now, for heaven's sake, let's get on our way quickly before I change my mind!"

He paused in the doorway and looked at her ashamedly, seeing the misery in her face.

"I've had affairs with other women since I married Harriet, but it's meant nothing to them or to me! If it's any consolation to you, Elizabeth, you're the first one I've had any finer feelings about at the last moment! Come on, my darling, please! Before I find it impossible to leave after all."

He took her gently by the arm, and silently they walked from the room. It was nearly midnight when Peter drew up outside her house. She stopped him as he took her case.

"No, don't come with me. Simon's often been away before, and I don't mind an empty house. I'll be all right, Peter."

As she turned the key in the front door, she became aware of a light in the lounge shining into the hall. Even as she sucked her breath in fear, Simon was there, anxious and distraught.

"Simon!' she said. "I thought you were in Manchester!"

"Where's Lucy?" he demanded. "Isn't she with you? Where have you been until this time of the night?"

"She's staying with Ella for the weekend. Why are you here, Simon? Why did you come back?"

He was staring at her suitcase.

"I called in at the office before I caught the train North, and a telegram had just arrived, cancelling the meeting until next week. I've been dreadfully worried since I came home, Elizabeth, because I knew you wouldn't keep Lucy out as late as this."

He gestured enquiringly towards the suitcase.

"Why did you take that?"

She said simply: "I was going away with Peter for the weekend."

"What the hell do you mean!" he exploded. "You're not serious!"

She stepped into the hall and shut the door, watching the disbelief in his dark eyes change to anger.

"I couldn't help it . . . " she began.

"I suppose it was bigger than both of you!" he interrupted.

She flinched.

"Simon, I'll try to explain why I went away with him, if you'll let me. Nothing came of it. We had dinner and then came home—Peter said I would regret it always."

The silence seemed endless before Simon asked: "And would you have?"

"Yes," she said frozenly. "I'm that sort of person, I suppose."

He turned towards her, and she saw the tension leave his face, as a possible explanation occurred to him. "You must have been tired, Elizabeth. You must have been very, very tired to have done this."

Her mind screamed at him, 'Won't you admit that I could be attractive to another man!'

Aloud, she said, "I wanted to go with Peter. It wasn't tiredness."

A strange expression came into his eyes as she asked him,

"Are you afraid to know that I have never really loved you?"

"I've always known it," he said simply. "I'm not a fool, Elizabeth." Tiredly, he added: "I don't blame you. You're a very lovely woman, and I knew you were attracted to Peter. I . . . I just hoped I had enough of your love to hold you. And there was Lucy, of course . . ."

She was deeply moved by the sincerity in his voice. "You've been very understanding," she said gently, "and I'm grateful. Please go on helping me, Simon. I need you."

She touched his arm as she moved away, and he watched her as she walked quietly towards the stairs. Unutterably weary, she longed only for sleep to strengthen her for a new day. And for all the days to come.

The Beautiful One

First published 24th February 1968
Woman's Weekly

Sometimes, a girl can be too beautiful. There is a quality about perfection that can frighten a man as much as it can attract. Jill was one of those girls. Her face was oval, without the faintest hint of a wrinkle; her eyes mirrored a sweetness and gentle femininity; her hair gleamed with fascinating lights. Her figure was Grecian, her skin was Dresden, and her voice was liquid honey. An embarrassment of riches for any one girl to possess, as Jill knew to her cost. She shared a flat with Fiona, who was quite pretty in a blonde, sweetly-rounded way, and very popular. Whenever the phone rang, which it did frequently, the voice, if it was male, always asked for Fiona.

It was on one of these occasions, as Fiona put down the receiver after gaily accepting an invitation to a meal out, that Jill gave a heavy sigh and slumped down on a chair, looking sad and beautiful in her pale blue housecoat. Fiona looked at her friend with compassion in her baby-blue eyes.

"I could easily get Keith to make up a foursome," she ventured.

Jill shook her head. "You know what happened when Colin brought a friend last time. I—I seem to scare them. At least, I scare the nice ones, and I just don't like the wolves!"

"Well, let me ring Keith," Fiona pleaded. "I can't bear the idea of your sitting at home while I go out."

She stared gloomily at the lovely creature cradling a pillow in her arms, as though it were a buffer from the cruel world.

"You must give men an inferiority complex. They just can't live up to you!"

"I've tried being motherly." Jill said.

"You don't look the motherly type," Fiona pointed out reasonably.

"Well, I've tried being gay and abandoned, too!"

"Yes, but you're the kind of person who can only be that with someone who brings out the best in you. Apparently you have to be almost in love to start being yourself.

"And Wonder Man could turn up at any time!" sighed Jill, good-humouredly. "All right, Fiona, ring Keith and ask him to bring a friend along with him."

At eight-thirty that evening Jill answered the door. She looked dazzling in a short dress of black velvet, with long sleeves of black lace. Keith stared at her, as a child might stare at a cream gateau, or a collector at a butterfly. Then he introduced his friend, Arthur, a quiet, pale, studious-looking man in his late twenties, who looked at Jill courteously, without too obviously scrutinizing her. His eyes were hidden behind horn-rimmed spectacles and his handshake was very slightly limp, but his manners were impeccable. Over dinner, he proved to be an amusing conversationalist, and Jill felt she had at last found someone who credited her with feelings and intelligence.

In the cloakroom, after dinner, Fiona applied her lipstick. "Like him?"

"I think so," Jill murmured. "He doesn't exactly thrill me, but I know I mustn't be too choosy."

"Well. darling, you're twenty seven and you don't want to be a secretary all your life!" said Fiona cheerfully. "Arthur's not at all bad-looking, and I've heard he's got bags of money stacked away."

"No one could possibly ask for more!" Jill agreed in mock seriousness.

Fiona glanced suspiciously at her friend, but Jill's lovely eyes were innocent and guileless in the perfect oval face.

"Ah, here you are!" Keith greeted them. "Arthur wants us to go round to his flat."

"Do come. It's right at the top of Milton Buildings, and there's a wonderful view over the City," Arthur said, joining them.

A silent lift deposited them in the carpeted corridor, and Jill began to believe Fiona's remark about bags of money. Arthur opened a cream-painted door, and ushered them into a wide hall, leading to an elegant lounge. Two women sat on a brocade settee, and the younger one rose, and walked across to them.

"Arthur, you've brought some friends home. How nice!"

"Mother and Betsy, I want you to meet Fiona, Jill and Keith," said Arthur.

His sister and mother smiled in acknowledgement, and then their smiles froze a little as they saw Jill's exquisite face.

"Do sit down," they said, while their eyes followed Jill, not quite believing that one female should possess so much beauty. "Arthur will pour us some drinks."

They chatted to their guests, and showed the superb view from their balcony, but again and again their eyes returned, as if mesmerized, to Jill, and she could feel their unspoken worry that their beloved Arthur might be lured away by this enchantress! She knew Arthur liked her, and now she understood his faintly old-fashioned mannerisms. She smiled to herself, for to take Arthur away from this silver-haired woman and her daughter, would be like depriving flowers of the sun! Arthur was talking to her, his gentle, scholarly face kind and attentive.

"There is a difference of ten years between Betsy and me," he said. "Mother has been married twice, and I was born when she was thirty-five. My father died last year."

Jill looked at him and knew intuitively that he was content with his life and did not need her sympathy. He had the adulation of his female household, and he was a completely happy man.

"Why is it," she asked Fiona later, as the girls drank their hot chocolate before going to bed, "that when I at last meet a man who demands nothing of me except to be myself, I find I would have to compete with his mother and his sister?"

She stared unseeingly at a bowl of scarlet tulips lighting a dark corner of their small comfortable lounge.

"It's April!" she said suddenly. "I need a change. I want to look at the sun on the sea, to hear the gulls, and walk along the cliffs."

"Well, you've got a sister living near Polperro," suggested Fiona.

"Exactly!" Jill said. "What am I waiting for? The office owes me four days, and I can tack them onto the weekend, so Cornwall, here I come!"

The train snaked out of Paddington, and Jill leaned back against her seat, watching the close-built backs of the houses change slowly to the dappled pattern of the spring fields.

By the time she arrived at the small country station, she was satiated with glimpses of Easter lambs, and grassy embankments revealing the curdled cream of primroses.

Her sister, Helen, tweed suited and efficient, with clear brown eyes and a fresh-air complexion, greeted her with delight.

"Lovely to see you. You don't visit us enough, my dear, and you know how we love having you."

The farmhouse atmosphere was enveloping and complete; home-baked bread, dairy butter and rich clotted cream. Jill slept dreamlessly, and awoke to shafted sunlight and the smell of bacon and mushrooms. She listened drowsily to Sandy, her brother-in-law singing as he shaved, and she visualized the small Cornish harbour where she had decided to spend the morning. It had pink and white houses covering the cliff-side down to the rocks, and moored boats slapping gently in the green water.

Soon, she was walking down the narrow main street, and everything was as it had been on her last visit two years ago. Gulls swooped over cottages that were fondant-coloured in the translucent light from the water, and quaint shops getting ready for the summer season. She knew most of the villagers, and it was nearly midday before she reached the end of the street leading down to the harbour.

Suddenly her eyes were held by some paintings exhibited in a small shop window, and she was immediately entranced by their clarity and beauty. They were all local scenes, and she joyfully recognized Sandy's farm, high on the cliffs. She bent her head as she went through the tiny doorway, and closed her eyes for a moment at the contrast of the dark interior to the bright April sunshine outside. When she opened them, she saw a tall man in a fisherman's jersey watching her silently. She could not know that his impassivity at that moment hid an emotion that rendered him quite speechless. Peter Tremayne had answered the call of his shop doorbell without knowing that he was about to see a creature that could make even a mermaid look like an accompaniment to vinegar and chips!

"Where is Mr Tremayne?" Jill asked.

Peter gulped. "Mr Tremayne? He's retired and I've taken over. He's my uncle."

"Does he still live in Polperro?"

"Yes, he has a cottage across the harbour."

She smiled. "I would like to see a painting in your window. It's of my brother-in-law's farm, and if it's not too expensive I want to buy it for my sister. I'm staying with her, you see . . ."

Jill's voice trailed away, because for some reason, her heart was pounding away so hard that she was breathless.

The young man had moved from the darkness towards the window, and she saw the width of his shoulders in the old sweater, a calm mouth, and dark, crisp hair. He was pleasant and courteous while he showed her the paintings, revealing that he was, in fact, the artist.

"They're really splendid," she said, as he wrapped her purchase. "You've had training?"

"For a while," he smiled. "But I'm basically lazy, and I couldn't stand the idea of a job in town, so I invested in a small motor launch with some money left to me, and now I take visitors around the headland, and I fish, and I sell my paintings."

"It sounds lovely," murmured Jill. "And I wouldn't call it lazy!"

She moved away with her parcel, and urgency impelled him to say; "How long are you staying here?"

"About a week."

She hesitated, because she didn't want to leave, but he said no more, and with a vague feeling of disappointment she left the little shop.

Peter sat down slowly, and groped for his pipe. After a while, he locked the shop and rowed across the harbour to his uncle's cliffside cottage.

"Oh, that would be Jill Baxter," said John Tremayne. "Yes, I know her well. She'll be calling to see me, for sure." He poured some cider into two tankards. "You want some advice?"

Peter said nothing.

"Well, even if you don't, I'll give it to you! She's too beautiful, boy. A beautiful woman should be avoided. Perfection is dangerous. Anyhow, she's probably got more men friends than you can count, where she comes from."

Peter slumped visibly as the truth of this last statement struck him with crushing force.

"Still," said his uncle, comfortingly, "you've had so many girlfriends that I doubt if that would worry you."

"This one's different," said Peter, and the old man chuckled.

"I mean it!" insisted his nephew. "She's beautiful, but somehow she also looks sad and vulnerable. Honestly, Uncle, I would have said she was lonely, if it weren't for the fact that she's so lovely."

"Well, I've known her since she was seventeen, when her sister came to live here, and she's always been pretty enough to turn every man's head. Perhaps she's just had a broken love affair. That might account for her looking sad," suggested John Tremayne.

Peter rowed thoughtfully back across the harbour and, as he moored at the small jetty, he saw Jill sitting on a capstan, watching some fishermen hauling in the mackerel nets. Resolutely he moved towards her, then he paused and felt in his jacket for his sketching pad. She was staring down at the fishermen, her chin cupped in one hand, her hair tumbling down each side of her face. Her short, tweed skirt. and golden sweater against the grey harbour walls and azure sky, made

39

him catch his breath. For ten minutes he worked intently, then as she rose to go, turning behind her to pick up the painting she had bought from him, she saw him.

"Hallo," she said, gravely. "I love watching them bring in the fish. It's all so timeless and peaceful."

"I've just been to see my uncle." He fell into step beside her. "He said he's looking forward to your visit."

"Of course. I wouldn't go back to London without seeing him."

"I always found life in London a bit hectic." He spoke casually.

Equally casual, she replied, "Yes, we have a pretty mad time." Miserably, she wondered why she had lied.

Impulsively, Peter said; "I'm taking the launch out for a trial run tomorrow. She's just been overhauled for the season. Would you like to come?"

Early next morning, they headed out to an island down the coastline, where the only inhabitants were large and very disapproving seagulls. Peter had provided a picnic lunch, and there was crusty farm bread, and golden butter, and a curd tart from Jill's sister. They found a cove, warm in the pale sun, sheltered from the chill breeze, and they relaxed, content after chicken and salad and wine. Peter put away his sketching pad, and raised himself on his elbow.

"Do you really have a mad time, living in London, Jill?"

"No," she said, because she knew, now, that with this man she must be utterly sincere.

"Are you in love with anyone?"

"No," she said again. "And no man has ever been in love with me."

"I can't believe that," he said, almost angrily.

She sat up, looking impossibly beautiful in her navy slacks and white sweater. "It's true. I scare them, I think." She stared across the silver sands. "They imagine that because—because—"

"Because you're so lovely," he prompted gently.

"Well, I suppose they imagine that I'm always going to run around with other men!"

40

He didn't reply, and she turned to look at him. He was sitting with his hands clasped around his knees, and suddenly all she wanted in the world was for him to hold her close. His eyes were dark and expressionless in his tanned face.

"I was married," he said. "Her name was Catherine. She was drowned two and a half years ago in a sudden squall off this coast."

He stood up with a restless, impatient movement, and stared down at Jill, his hands in his pockets.

"Don't sympathise," he said, as she started to speak. "She was on the point of leaving me. She was in love with another man and it was from his yacht that she was drowned."

He picked up a stone and threw it at a nearby rock.

"I'm not going to dramatize this," he said. "We were out of love, so I was probably equally to blame."

He smiled drily. "If there was any excuse for either of us, we were both very young!"

"She was beautiful?" asked Jill, slowly.

"Yes," he said. "But there it ended! She cared for no one but herself."

He held out his hand, and when she stood beside him, he put his arm around her shoulders, but only said; "Let's get back to the mainland. The tide is just right."

He picked up the picnic basket, and until they reached the harbour, they hardly spoke a word. In the dusk, he drove her back to the farm in his Land-Rover, and walked with her up the curving driveway. Where the shadows joined the lights of the house, he turned her towards him, and kissed her gently. For a long moment, she clung to him, and then he left her, and she heard him start the car and drive away.

The day before Jill was to return to London, Helen went into the barn to collect some eggs. A stifled sob made her look round anxiously, and she saw her sister sitting on an upturned barrel. Silently she walked across the stone floor.

"It's Peter, isn't it, Jill? Why don't you go down to the harbour and see him?"

Violently, Jill shook her head. "I couldn't do that. Don't you see, Helen, it's the same thing that's happening all the time. I've scared him off. His wife was the same as me, and he dare not make another mistake. He wouldn't be able to trust me."

"Now, listen to me!" Helen said gently. "Firstly, you don't scare Peter Tremayne that easily—he's not the type! Secondly, his wife was not the same as you. Beautiful maybe, but flint and ice underneath."

"Then why hasn't he called to see me?" asked Jill, tearfully.

Helen wilted a little. "I honestly don't know," she confessed.

The following morning, Helen and Sandy sat gloomily at their breakfast table, listening to the sound of packing from Jill's bedroom.

"I feel like telling young Tremayne what a fool he is," growled Sandy. "He's got to be in love with her!"

"But he isn't a fool, Sandy, that's what I can't understand. He's had to learn such a hard lesson about beautiful women that I'm sure his experience would enable him to see at once what a darling Jill is, despite her perfect face."

Sandy gulped his coffee. "Well, perhaps the whole affair embittered him more than any of us realised."

An hour later, talking to Jill on the platform, Sandy's sensitive ears detected the sound of a Land-Rover tearing down the station approach, and he interrupted Jill in mid-sentence.

"I must rush now, my dear. It's been wonderful having you, and I know we'll be seeing you soon again."

Before she could say goodbye, Sandy vanished, and another figure, carrying a large parcel, was running towards her. The train had already drawn into the station, but she was quite unaware of anything but a great happiness as a paint-spattered Peter took her in his arms and kissed her, then pushed her into a carriage and deposited the parcel on her lap. He slammed the door.

"But, Peter, wait!"

He waved, as the train shunted out.

"You bet I will," he shouted. "Forever!"

Jill sat down and tore open the parcel, then gasped in delight, oblivious of the curious passengers. The painting was of herself, her long hair in two straight curtains each side of her oval face, with the affinity of sea and sky caught in heavenly blues and greens around her.

Above all, shining through the beauty which Peter had captured so surely, was the unmistakeable glow and warmth of a woman deeply in love.

Fool's Paradise

First published 10th March 1984
Woman's Own

Johnny doesn't like depression or illness or bad news. So I am always bright and healthy. I have my hang-ups and my headaches in quiet corners and, when Johnny walks into my flat, I am welcoming and happy.

"Come on," he says. "We'll have a picnic on the river. I've brought wine and Italian grapes."

As I reach for my new straw hat, I discard my plan to catch up on the backlog of weekend chores. He is watching me, leaning with his hand against the door frame, and I know that I please him.

"Nice hat," he says. "I like it."

"It's a traditional panama," I tell him. "Everyone's got one. It's made from the leaves of Ecuadorian pine."

"Now you're boring me," he groans. "Are you ready?"

"I'm ready," I reply, for I never keep Johnny waiting.

While we have our picnic, screened by April willows on the riverbank, I tell him that my firm is sending me to Devon on a public relations course. He bites into a chicken drumstick.

"You'll like Devon. How long for?"

In the same tone he has just said: "The wine's very good. I must put some by."

"About ten days. I go on Thursday." My pride prevents me from adding: 'You could easily take a few days off. Won't you come too?'

I drink my wine, then stretch out on my back, turning my head to watch the water-geese fussing their feathers on the opposite bank. They open their beaks in soundless indignation at a passing boat. Johnny wipes his hands and holds the grapes against my face. As I taste the scented juice I

44

forget my resentment. Johnny is here, on a green bank, warm in my arms; and while he is with me there are no shadows. As he eases his body over mine, a cabin cruiser comes round the bend of the river. Johnny curses.

"Ah, well, there's always tonight. Or is Jill monopolising your bedroom?"

I brush willow leaves from my hair. "Afraid so. She's invited her latest boyfriend and I've promised to keep out of the way."

He shrugs. "You've got yourself a promiscuous little flatmate."

"She's not really. She just hasn't found the right man yet."

"She'll never be satisfied, Nan. She's a modern day Salome."

"You're being unfair, Johnny."

"No, dimwit, I'm not. I've met her enough times to recognise her type.'

I think of Jill's lazy eyes and secret smile, and realise he is right. It will need a very special man to tame that perverse spirit. Johnny stands, looking down at me.

"You'd better come and stay with me, if Jill doesn't want you around. I'll drive you to work tomorrow."

I've kept an assortment of skirts and tops at Johnny's flat, since we became lovers four months ago. On that freezing night we had eaten a wine and spaghetti supper in front of the fire. Outside, my car succumbed to drifting snow; everything was cloaked and buried. 'Like Johnny's life,' I thought. I was beginning, even then, to know something of his mind. In his discovery of my inexperience, Johnny could have shown both arrogance and impatience. Yet, to is credit, that night he had overcome my fear to make each heightened moment a sharing.

"Come on, Nan! Stir yourself, girl!"

I wake from my daydream and start packing the cool-bag. The evening river is sparked with light as we row back to the boatyard and walk to the car park. Johnny is in high spirits and I respond to his teasing, knowing instinctively that my ten-day course in Devon will not be mentioned again.

Later, in the aftermath of loving, Johnny tells me we are a great partnership, and I reciprocate his praise. I have learned my lesson well since the day when I said to him:

"We could be so happy together."

We had been sprawled on my sitting-room carpet, looking at the Sunday papers, a large coffee-pot between us. He had raised his head before resuming his reading.

"We are happy together, dummy."

"I mean together for always, Johnny."

"Forget it, Nan."

His voice was gentle. "Live for now. If you're content, that's enough."

I had persisted. "Don't you believe in marriage?"

"No."

If I had known him then as I do now, I would have recognised the warning on his face. Abruptly he had risen, throwing aside the paper.

"Where are you going?" I asked, still not understanding.

His reply was cold.

"To the pub."

And he was gone.

In the five days before I saw him again, I had wisely decided to come to terms with our relationship rather than lose him.

The day before I leave for Devon, Johnny calls at my flat. For a moment I wonder if he is coming with me, but he simply tells me he has tickets for a Tom Stoppard play at the end of the month. While he is having a drink, Jill appears from the bathroom. Her Janet Reger mini-wrap emphasises every curve of her lovely body as she glances indifferently at Johnny. He raises his whisky glass to her mockingly while his eyes move slowly down her brown legs. Then he turns from her and pours himself another drink.

Late that night, Jill talks to me as she manicures her nails in the bed next to mine.

"You'll not change him, Nan. Why try?"

46

"Because I want something permanent, I suppose. Don't all women?"

"Not necessarily. Lots don't."

She leans across to pat my shoulder as she reaches to her bedside lamp.

"Accept him as he is, Nan, or you'll lose him. I think you're much too nice for him anyway."

I smile, my confidence unshaken.

"Oh, he'll change for me one day."

She stares at me for a moment with her strange, dark eyes; then she switches off the light and slides under her duvet.

On the drive to the coast, I see swathes of primroses on the sunny perimeters of the woods, and I find my hotel situated on a green-water bay. Despite myself, I feel somehow exhilarated.

The first eight days of the course are absorbing, and I almost forget that Johnny has not phoned me. I know he must be busy. As I study the programme for the last two days, I realise I will be going over old ground, and I make an impulsive decision to return to London in the evening. I ring Jill to tell her of my plans, adding that I will drive direct to Johnny's flat.

"He approves of surprises," I say, "so I won't let him know."

As I replace the receiver, I see us drinking champagne and making love in his king-size bed.

It takes longer than I think to negotiate the City traffic, and when I open the flat door with the key I always carry, I see it is a quarter-past eleven. I call Johnny's name. Almost immediately, he appears from the bedroom in his underpants, switching on the light and staring at me with blank eyes.

"Good God, Nan, you said you wouldn't be home until next Monday!"

"That's no welcome for a tired traveller." I kiss him.

He catches my arm and, before I realise what is happening, we are in the kitchen, drinking coffee.

"Look, Nan, I've got one hell of a day at the office tomorrow. I'll be closeted with old Jennings for hours on his new project."

"That's all right," I yawn. "Just set the alarm for me when you get up. Wearily, I push back my chair. "Let's go to bed."

I walk towards the bedroom, but Johnny is there before me.

"I mean it, Nan. I'd rather you didn't stay."

Bewildered by his tone, I gape at him. Then a drowsy voice calls:

"Johnny? What's going on?"

Over his shoulder in the bedroom doorway, I see the familiar wisp of creamy silk, the lovely curves and the dark, tousled hair.

"You should have done as I asked, Nan." Johnny sounds irritated rather than worried. "Then you wouldn't have been hurt."

My eyes return to Jill, and I experience a rage at her calm appraisal, which helps to steady my treacherous voice.

"Why should I be hurt, Johnny? We're both free."

As I bend to pick up my case, I pause, remembering suddenly how he cherishes his privacy.

"Just one more thing," I say, my humiliation sweetened by revenge. "If you're going to go on sleeping with Jill, move her in here permanently will you? I don't want her in my flat."

I move across the room, hoping the tears won't come before I reach the merciful dark of the stairs. In final defiance, I say:

"Don't ever try to get in touch with me. I mean it."

He shrugs. "If that's how you want it, Nan."

His unrepentant answer triggers in me an emotion that I do not at once recognise as the blossoming of my new freedom, although gradually I am becoming conscious of a sense of release. As I open the door, I catch a glimpse of Jill's face in a wall mirror and, for the first time that night, I remember that she had known I was coming. I see her slow, secret smile. But I didn't look back.

Close Friends

First published 7th September 1985
Woman's Own

Richard says, 'This is Anna,' and I take the outstretched hand. Because she is tall, with fine proportions, I am surprised by the soft fingers and delicate bones. Her voice is low-pitched and husky.

"I feel I already know you, Lindy."

I try not to stare at her—at that beautiful olive skin and black curtain of hair. I sense a loneliness about her, yet she seems confident, with a direct and steady gaze. She is still speaking.

"So you're staying in Richard's cramped lodgings?" The words are conventional, but I am sure her question shows concern.

"No rooms at college for second years." I tell her. "I suppose I was one of the lucky ones, having a brother to move in with."

Richard turns to Anna.

"She hasn't mentioned I've given her my room!" he says wryly. "I'm having to share with Steve, in a four-by—six floor space."

"Stop being a martyr," I say, with sisterly affection. "You won't have to put up with me for very much longer. I'll soon find another place."

I realise, suddenly, that my hand has remained in hers during this entire exchange and that she is gently releasing it. The uncertainty which has been with me these past few months makes me want to return to the strength and warmth of her clasp. Instead, I say,

"You're an artist and a very good one, according to Richard."

Anna shrugs.

"Just hoping for a future in commercial design," she says, "and an employer who might believe in me. No harm in reaching for the moon, even if it's from the doorway of the jobcentre!"

She seats herself on a chair covered in green silk tapestry. I think how right she looks in the setting of the lovely room. Richard taps her on the arm.

"Stop being such a cynic," he tells her, pretending to be stern. "They won't be able to hold out against your talent for much longer."

"Keep on telling me that, will you?" she says. "It does help to compensate for all that endless form-filling."

"Anyway, Anna, it's you and me both—one engineer and one artist; have degrees; try anything."

He is determinedly bright. Then he notices me, looking on curiously.

"You're wondering what an out of work Anna is doing in rooms like these, with carpets and velvet curtains, eh, Lindy?"

I examine a water-colour on a nearby wall.

"And originals instead of posters!" I feel vaguely nervous, knowing Anna is watching me, and I automatically straighten my shoulders.

"Prosperous cousin goes for a cruise," Richard elaborates. "Knew Anna was job hunting. Lends her the place for three months."

He indicates, with a sweep of his head.

"There's a large bathroom on a separate level, fitted kitchen and mezzanine sitting room . . .'

"Hey! I'm sitting right here," Anna objects. "I'm a big girl, Richard. I can do my own talking."

He is contrite. As he stoops down to give her a brief hug, I notice that, almost imperceptibly, she draws away. "Sometimes," she says, "Richard does rather underestimate our basic abilities. I imagine he plays the big brother, too, doesn't he, Lindy?"

"Guards me as fiercely as a Doberman," I laugh.

Richard has set himself on the arm of her chair and is still admiring the room.

"Anna, love, how about having a party here? Would your cousin mind?"

She accepts the question with nonchalance.

"I think she anticipated it. She's put her Capodimonte and Rockingham in safe deposit."

Richard is impressed.

"What a sensible woman."

At the party, the music is good and constant throughout the evening. Richard has laid on some Bulgarian wine, which is far better than I thought it would be at the price he paid for it. Halfway through the evening, I am talking to Anna in a corner of the room.

"I didn't know you were as friendly as that with Steve," she is saying, above the noise. "I thought it was just Richard who knew him well."

She looks over at the young man who is plying some giggling girls with slices of pizza. My reply is rushed and over-explanatory.

"Steve's at the same college as me. He's a third-year student, and we only go out together occasionally. It's all very casual, but we have fun."

"He's extremely attracted to you," she points out.

"He's attracted to all females!" I assure her.

There is something quizzical in her expression which makes me defensive.

"He's never turned me on, if that's what you mean."

Her voice is quiet.

"I'm sorry, Lindy. I wasn't meaning to pry."

Someone is signalling to her from the other side of the room.

"I'd better go and see who wants coffee."

She grimaces, her eyes still apologetic, and moves towards the buffet table. I am dismayed when Steve leaves his admiring circle and strolls over to me.

"Haven't seen much of you tonight, Lindy."

"Sorry about that," I say. "But you were always hedged in."

"Yeah, well, that's the way I am!" He takes my elbow. "It's a bit stuffy in here, isn't it? Like some fresh air?"

"There's a small roof garden," I tell him. "I'll get my jacket."

He is intrigued as we go through the beautiful kitchen.

"Do I hear the rattle of money-bags?"

I open the door leading to the patio.

"A twice removed rattle. Anna has a rich cousin."

We lean on a stone balustrade. The distant lamps by the river star the darkness, and we hear the muted roar of London's traffic. Steve is close enough for me to feel the heat of his shoulder, and I observe with detached interest that he is edging even closer. His speech is slurred. I guess he has been going heavily at the Bulgarian wine to gain courage for his customary persuasive tactics when we are alone together, and which I had not revealed to Anna earlier on. I sense that his hand is sliding around my breast. I move away from him.

"Oh, come on, Lindy." He glares at me, unpleasantly intense. "What's up with you? Worried about your exams or something?"

"Why do you ask?" He peers into my face, trying hard to focus on me. "Because you're acting like even more of an iceberg than usual."

I turn to him.

"Next term isn't going to be easy. I've got to go above a simple pass if I'm to be in the running for a job. It makes me uncertain about everything."

He frowns, thrusting his hands into his denims and rocking on his heels.

"Okay, so you're mixed-up. Aren't we all?"

"I'm not mixed-up, Steve."

His attitude is beginning to annoy me. He ignores my remark.

"You know I'd like you to sleep with me?"

"Yes, I know. You've asked me often enough."

"Well, why don't you?"

"I don't want to."

Although I speak with forced calmness, I have to resist a desire to laugh at the expression of perplexity on his face.

"Why can't we just be friends," I ask.

"You must be joking! I'm a normal guy with normal appetites—you won't get me tying myself up with a moral miss like Anna who won't . . . Okay, I'm not as patient as Richard; but I want you, Lindy . . ."

He steps nearer, confident I won't resist. I evade him and step quickly into the shadowed kitchen.

Anna is standing in the doorway, reaching for the light-switch.

"Party's over," she says. "Wine's run out! And I'm about to make some coffee."

Steve stalks past us, and I speak on impulse.

"Anna, could I stay tonight? I can sleep on the settee."

"Certainly you shall stay. The settee is a put-you-up, incidentally, which I have always wanted to try, so you can have my room."

She holds up her hand to silence my protests.

"I insist, Lindy. It's time you had a change from Richard's cubby-hole."

"I couldn't. Why should you.?"

"Wait until you see the luxury of it," she interrupts me. "There's a bathroom-en-suite, and it's even got a sunken bath!"

I weaken. "I don't believe it. Could I go up now please?"

She laughs at my eagerness.

The room is a candy-floss haven of silk shades and fluffy rugs. We make up the bed with pink pillow-cases and a matching duvet cover. Outside on the landing, she pauses. She is wearing something in gypsy colours which complements her sun-browned skin and ebony hair. I am clumsy in my Indian cotton skirt and loose top, and I shift my feet under her amused gaze. Slowly, she reaches to stroke my reddening cheek.

"You look like a night-gowned child," she says. "I should read you a bed-time story."

Before I can reply, she continues: "I heard everything between you and Steve this evening."

She watches me.

"When you asked if you could stay the night, you forestalled me by about two seconds." She turns away. "Goodnight, Lindy. Sleep well."

Long after she has gone, I stand there, looking at shadows. Later, when I tell Richard that I'm to share Anna's flat until I find other accommodation, he doesn't seem surprised.

"Fine. Sounds like a good arrangement." He hesitates. "What do you think of Anna?"

"I think she's great. I'd hardly be moving in with her otherwise."

"I guess not." Richard sound thoughtful. "She's got personality, that's for sure. But she's introspective, deep."

"What do you mean?" I speak with unwarranted sharpness.

"Well, she's not exactly outgoing, is she? I suppose you've realised I want her to marry me?"

I hadn't.

"You see, I'm short-listed for a job. Construction engineering. I haven't got it yet, so I've only told you and Anna. If I land it, she'll have no more excuses to put me off. I'd be earning enough for both of us. She could still dabble in art."

"Dabble!' I am furious. "She intends to make art her livelihood."

"But isn't marriage what most girls prefer?" he asks. "Isn't it what they need?"

"Correction. It's what most men like to *think* girls need!"

He walks to the door. "Aggressive today, aren't you?" he says.

He looks at me for a moment before he leaves, but says nothing.

So now I have been with Anna for nearly a week, and Richard has started his course at Harrogate. We share so much happiness, Anna and I; so much laughter. I don't think about forthcoming end-of—term assessments. Nor do I think of Anna's cousin, who is due back within the month. I live for the minute, with each day bringing heightened experiences and a growing sensation of belonging. She speaks to me with lover's words. She tells me my face is acutely sensitive, and that the small gap between my front teeth, which I have always hated, is sensual and appealing.

She makes me conscious of my every movement. I feel happy and assured, always anxious that she should approve of me. She comes into the bedroom one day as I am brushing my hair. She stands behind me.

"Alice in Wonderland must have looked at you."

She catches my long hair and winds it upwards.

"I want to sketch your portrait. Wear your hair like this."

I study her features in the mirror.

"You're beautiful, Anna, "I say. "There is such strength in your face."

A few days later, I casually mention to Anna that a boy called John has asked me out to a meal the next day. Without looking at me, she says,

"It's up to you. Why consult me? You can do what you choose."

I enjoy the evening. John is calm and undemanding, with a dry wit. Towards the week's end, we go up to the theatre. Anna is waiting up, when I get back to the flat after midnight.

"I was worried," she said, sitting tall and straight in the chair.

"There was no need, Anna, I went for a beer to John's rooms."

"Was that wise?'

"What are you saying?"

"Why do you imagine he asked you back?"

I feel suddenly resentful.

"You think I went to bed with him?"

She is scornful.

"Well, you weren't just sitting, drinking beer. Don't lie, Lindy. I'm sure he couldn't wait to get his hands on you."

"I don't have to tell you anything." She is silent, staring at me with her dark unfathomable eyes. I stand there, my defiance ebbing; then I am in her arms, and she is holding me, soothing and comforting me like a child. For the next ten days, she fills and satisfies my life. When I return each evening from my research in the college library, she has prepared a tempting meal; or we lunch at an Italian restaurant, walking home along the towpath, where the gulls scavenge the cold, grey river and the east wind bites at our faces. Sometimes, we visit the opera, which Anna is teaching me to appreciate. She buys new clothes for me. Finally I protest:

"I can't let you do this." I am holding a black cashmere sweater, which I could never have afforded for myself. "You're out of work," I continue. "You don't have the money to spend on such lovely things."

She smiles.

"I have a generous allowance from my father—more than I need."

The nerves in my stomach tighten. I am beginning to feel as stifled as I was with Steve, although I keep trying to push my fears aside . . .

The next time I arrange to meet John, I don't tell Anna. After that I find it easier not to tell her of further meetings—and certainly not to tell her I have found, with him, a quiet acceptance of me, as I am. Yet I cannot bring myself to leave her, although my feelings for her are now mingled with irritation. I lie to her that I have to study in the evenings even though I l know she doesn't believe me.

At breakfast one morning, she asks, suddenly,

"Tell me, is anything wrong?"

I select an apple from the fruit bowl, rolling it round my palm with the other hand, playing for time.

"I didn't think you'd notice."

"I notice when you're unhappy, Lindy. Of course I do."

I bite into the apple. I want to protest that I resent her awareness of my every mood. She knows my thistledown days and the days when I am depressed. She knows the sum and the substance of my life-force. I merely say,

"How can you tell I am not happy?"

She cradles her coffee cup. She humours me.

"Your feet don't turn out any more when you walk!" she tells me teasingly.

Impatiently, I throw away my half eaten fruit. "Don't joke, Anna. I suppose you've guessed that . . ." I decide to soften the blow, " . . . that I'm getting restless."

Her mouth is controlled.

"Fair enough, Lindy. We haven't been out for a while. Let's do something different."

"No!" I speak too quickly.

Carefully, she replaces her cup on its saucer and pushes her chair away from the table. She sits still, her hands in her lap.

"Why not? You say you are restless. You've probably been working too hard."

"It's not that, Anna. You don't understand."

Her eyes are bright, almost luminous. "Is this,—this student . . ."

"You mean John."

"Is he being troublesome?"

"No, Anna. He's really nice. We have fun."

"Like you used to have with Steve, I suppose?"

My reply is spurred by her derision.

"There's quite a difference. I wasn't in love with Steve!"

I hadn't meant to tell her until I was sure of myself. I had wanted to feed it to her gradually. In the silence, I avoid looking at her. Through the far window, the winter sky is skeined with violet, but I see it without pleasure, knowing that she is staring at me.

"Things will work out."

Her voice is cheerless. I stand, relieved to have the opportunity of leaving the room.

"By the way," she says, as I reach the doorway.

I stop and glance back at her. She keeps me waiting a fraction longer than I find comfortable.

"I've finished your portrait, Lindy. It's the best work I've ever done."

I nod, and quietly close the door, bewildered that she inevitably has the power to unnerve me. When we meet over supper, Anna tells me she has been interviewed that afternoon for a post in textile design. She gives me a word-picture of the personnel manager which is sharply observed and amusing. Yet her laughter has a harlequin-emptiness that I find deeply disturbing and I know that, if my emotions are to survive, I must make my decision. On the day that Richard is due home, I return in the evening to the flat. Anna has laid the table with infinite care. A solitary candle stand, rocket-sleek, on a base of white and yellow flowers, and she has floated some rose petals in two delicate finger-bowls.

"The table looks simply exquisite," I tell her.

She seems far away. "What?"

"The table, Anna, it's elegant."

She looks at me, then walks to the window and stares at nothing, her shoulders rounded because she is hugging her elbows. As I move towards the stairs, I barely hear the low voice.

"We'll eat when you're ready."

I pause, my hand on the stair-rail.

"No, Anna—not us. Perhaps you and Richard."

I keep my head averted and my words steady.

"John is picking me up in a few minutes to drive me to his place, for the time being."

The scent from the table-freesias is strong in the warm room as she comes towards me. I dare not turn in her direction, although I know she is standing near me. She speaks softly, but she doesn't touch me.

"You know I love you, Lindy."

"That's the trouble," I say, "you loved me too much."

"How can you be sure you're doing the right thing?"

I close my eyes, thinking of the laughter we've shared; the books. the food. the foreign films to which she's opened my eyes.

"Anna, I'm sorry. I shall never regret what we've had during these last weeks; but for me, it couldn't last."

Again, she asks, "How can you be sure?"

"I may never be, but lately I've lost so many of my doubts. Maybe, I've found myself. I just don't know."

I hesitate, certain she is willing me to stay.

"John is going to the States and I want to apply for a transfer to finish my studies over there. It's for the best, isn't it, Anna?'

The proud face turns away so that I shan't see her sadness and I go quickly to the bedroom to pack my holdall, leaving behind the clothes which Anna bought me. When I come back, she is sitting on the window-seat, her body motionless, her gaze now calm and impersonal.

I leave the room, halting on the cold landing, overwhelmed and almost frightened by my new freedom. Then, I begin to walk downstairs, feeling for each step, making sure my feet precisely match the pattern on the carpet, as I did when I was a child. The bell rings at the main door, and I start to hurry, the urgency of reaching the bottom becoming increasingly important; so that I can escape to a new day.

To Women

Do you remember the mornings of your world?
Light was everywhere. It never rained.
You, on the edge of life, were conscious of men
But conscious more of power, when one who thought
He was the hunter, hung in your silken web.

Do you remember flesh upon flesh, as seeking fingers
Met responsive limbs? That peacock boy, sequestered in
your lover
Craving your admiration, while trampling on your dreams?

Yet, men are less pretentious than their fathers, albeit prisoners,
Walled by their emotions. Frightened to give, lest, in the giving
They lose control of sensibility. For love transcends, almost
annihilates
The senses, and, at times, may stifle. This, men fear.

Women like things tidy. However huge the spectrum, they'll
compact it.
Men will divide and label, unless, by reason of their natures,
They're motivated, at this moment, by their passions.

A woman grows with love. Her life is nurtured by it.
If love is offered and she desires the giver,
She returns it hundredfold. It colours all her days.
Spurn her, she becomes a shrew. Reject her, she is loveless.

Unleash emotion by the honeyed word, the caring phrase,
And, if men speak them, therein lies their power.

Yet, still they hesitate. They see the curling tongue
Moisten the open lips; the heavy-lidded eyes;
The easy posture in the chair; the glimpse of thigh;
The instep arched; the hands quiescent, with upturned
palms.

They know that, in surrender, they are lost. Their wanting
Vies with clarity and reason. The spirit's bondage
Is the sun and substance, the razor's edge.

Man, born of woman, possessed by her, and loved.
And, by her silken threads, led to Golgotha.

A Weekend In Eden

First published 27th July 1985
Woman's Own

Strolling together, we bend our heads as we talk. I stop to pick blackberries, eating them with care and offering some to Fran. I look around me. The beech woods are heavy with summer leaves and the hedgerows are gleaming with various shades of green. I speak slowly, emphasising my words.

"I must be mad to live in London! Just why did I go there?"

She licks the corners of her lips with a stained tongue.

"Presumably because of your handsome Italian. You always were impetuous." There is no accusation in the gentle voice. She is stating a fact.

"I admit that," I say. "I really loved him at the time, though. Do you think I'm wiser since then?"

The clear eyes are warm and understanding.

"No—just more experienced!"

She eats the rest of her blackberries and wipes away the juice.

"But why use the past tense, Rosemary? I'm certain your feelings for him haven't changed."

I study her face, grateful to her for accepting me at a few days notice and for supplying hot chocolate and sympathy when I told her of my quarrel with Stefano. She had listened without interrupting, sitting curled and quiet, her hands calm as a nun's, with clasped fingers. As we move again towards the village, she is laughing because I am serious. Seeing her perfect teeth, I recall the ugly braces of her schooldays. She has never been beautiful, except when her smile transforms her. We reach a row of whitewashed houses and a church with a square tower. The general store is about to close and Fran rushes in, returning minutes later with a filled carrier bag. For a moment, we stand and watch rooks circle above the beeches. I take Fran's arm.

"Thank you for being here when I needed you."

With anyone else I would have had to elaborate. To tell them that, through their kindness and tolerance, I was becoming whole again. To Fran, I say no more. In two days we have recaptured the years when, like dark-haired sisters, we prowled the school, sharing our secrets.

Fran's stone-built house lies in a roll of hills, protected by a fruiting orchard. In the distance, a glint of gold marks the river boundary of the small farm. Inside, the dining table is laid with a red cloth. Over by the hearth a puppy stirs and yaps crossly in its sleep, a back leg twitching. As Fran disappears to the kitchen, declining my offer of help, a door slams and I turn to smile at the man who has entered the room. The puppy wakes and wags a stumpy tail, yawning and sighing and then settling once more to sleep.

"Had a good day?" asks Simon.

He passes my chair in his sober business suit, not waiting for a reply. He doesn't respond to my smile, but he continues to look at me as he picks up his mail and calls,

"Did you remember to put the wine in the fridge, Fran?"

There is a cry of despair from the kitchen.

"Oh. no, I forgot! It'll have to be red."

Her head appears, momentarily, in the doorway.

"Get a bottle out, will you, Simon? I'm beating eggs."

"Women!"

He throws the letters on the sideboard. I watch him as he stoops to the wooden rack beneath. He is tall and slim, with hair so perfectly cut it seems stitched to his well-shaped head. The eyes are penetrating and darkly-blue. They trouble me. Placing the wine on the table, he shouts in the direction of the kitchen.

"I'm going for a shower. Be down in ten minutes." His eyes are again on my face and I shiver although the room is warm. He touches my cheek as he leaves.

Fran's children come in, wearing the T-shirts I had brought them from London. They stand, all boys, in a solemn row of three, downgrading in height. Usually they are boisterous and argumentative; but at other, quieter times, they have their father's charm and their mother's gentleness. I see Fran in them now, questioning but also listening, with her mixture of concentration and gravity. I laugh at them.

"You're insatiable!" I say as I tell them again the story of Vesuvius erupting and of a town and its people being buried alive.

Fran enters with a steaming tureen.

"Call your father and wash your hands, in that order!"

As Simon opens the wine, the children sit at the table, impatient to eat but curbed by Fran's warning glance. Despite her mildness, she is a strict disciplinarian. Simon's fingers are lightly on my shoulder as he fills my glass and I feel the pressure long after he sits down. I notice that his wrists, although muscular, are not pencilled with dark hair like Stefano's; nor is his skin brown . . . and I become acutely conscious of the healthy redness of the faces around me in contrast to my own, still deeply tanned from my Italian holiday. The children all start to talk, unrestrainedly.

"I saw a bear in the fields!" cries the youngest, who invariably shouts to make himself heard.

Defiantly, he mashes potatoes into his meat while his brothers hoot in derision.

"It was a big dog! You never saw a bear!"

"I did too. I saw one!"

Fran ignores their argument.

"I do wish you could spend more time with us, Rosemary," she says.

"So do I." I am in complete agreement with her. "But I haven't been doing computer programming long enough to stay away from it. I was lucky to get even a few days."

I stop eating and look at her across the colourful expanse of bright tablecloth.

"Besides," I remind her, "you'll be back to teaching soon, and I'm sure you and Simon won't care to have me around the entire summer holiday."

I wait for his denial, but he has left us to put on a tape and doesn't seem interested in our conversation. When the children are in bed, Fran talks softly, recalling our teenage years. Simon prowls and fiddles with the video. He occasionally looks in our direction, as if resentful of our shared intimacy.

"Well, that was all a long time ago, Fran," he breaks in. "You're a big girl now."

She laughs up at him. I catch the expression in her grey eyes and I am ashamed of my envy. The room is fragrant with honeysuckle wafting through an open window. Fran and I make plans to take the children to the sea the next day.

"I've invited some friends for drinks tomorrow evening."

She rises to stretch, then squeezes my wrist in affection.

"They've asked to meet you, Rosemary. You've come from my past, you see."

Simon jabs, with unnecessary violence, at the video switch, his eyes hooded. I go up to the bedroom, warm under the eaves. I shut the door and lean against it, staring at the room made so welcoming for Fran's guests with its flower-patterned curtains contrasting so brightly with its white walls. It was such a happy and innocent room; a room where my emotions should not have been quite so diamond-hard, nor my body this eager and receptive.

I am aware that my mind is brittle with speculation and that what I feel now is exactly what I have been wanting to feel ever since the moment I arrived. I undress slowly, substituting action for disturbing thought.

At Fran's evening party, the women are friendly.

"How brown you are, Rosemary. That Amalfi coast . . ."

"The vivid colours. Aren't they just something?" "Did you go to Capri?" In the distance I see Simon leaning on one elbow on the mantle-shelf, talking to a group of men. I see the powerful muscles of his shoulders and arms flex under his shirt as he turns, just for a brief moment, towards me. Two hours before I had helped Fran feed and bed the protesting children after our day on the beach. After I'd finished showering and changing, I came down to the sitting room and stopped in the open door-way. Fran was standing with her back to me with Simon's arms around her, and, seeing me, he had deliberately moved his hand under her silk blouse while his eyes were directly at me over her head. As he continued to caress her, he watched me, his gaze insolent and faintly mocking. Quietly I had returned to the hall so that Fran would not know that I had witnessed their intimacy. I had stood out there for several minutes staring unseeingly at the opposite wall, fighting to curb an emotion I could not even understand.

Just then, women's voices intrude on my thoughts, drawing me back into their circle.

"Tell us about Herculaneum, Rosemary."

My mind still with the man on the other side of the room, I respond automatically to their questions and hear my own voice giving them the answers they want to hear.

Later Fran and I sip coffee and chat in low voices while Simon sprawls on the settee listening to the radio.

Fran searches for the shoes she has kicked off. She smiles lazily at us.

"Think I'll go on up. All that sea air today . . ."

She yawns before finishing the sentence and crosses the room, half-asleep, swinging her shoes. She pauses at the door to give us a floppy wave, and I glance down at my hands, observing in surprise that my fingers are clenched.

Simon turns off the radio and takes a cigar from the box on the table, then switches off the lamp, so the room becomes patterned with moonlight shining through the parted curtains. He looks at me. His expression is unreadable, and I realise he has set the scene and is now anticipating, with total confidence, that I will make the next move.

I leave my chair. I try to sound normal as I nod towards a corner, playing for time.

"You've got plenty of books over there, I see. I think I'll read in bed tonight."

He doesn't reply as I walk past him to take down a paperback, pretending to study it in the silver glow. He strikes a match, holding it to the end of his cigar. The smoke swirls around him, and he waits. Humiliation flushes my cheeks to crimson, as I glance through the pages, oblivious to their content, and make yet another random selection from the shelf. Then, finally and reluctantly, not quite knowing what else to do, I turn in the direction of the door.

Throwing his cigar into the fireplace, he is there before me, guiding me back into the centre of the room before I am even aware that he has done so. There is a practised ease, a total control, a lack of the obvious about his actions. I am lulled by an almost casual enjoyment, by the timeless, yet inexorable rhythm. All my longings of the past few weeks are channelled into immediacy, and it seems natural and right that I am the first to draw him closer, in a heightening of touch and sensation.

As his hands grow more urgent, I see over his shoulder the textures and the combinations of colour that make a home. On one pale wall, the painting of a reeded pool has Fran's tranquility. Chrysanthemums shine in a dark corner, flung just as they were picked into a decorative copper pot, perfect in their confusion. Beside them, Fran's workbasket is overflowing with the backlog of her children's mending. Fran is just as real in that peaceful room as if she were sitting, unruffled and cool, in the armchair.

I close my eyes; but it is too late to shut out the memory of watching Simon do to her what he is doing now to me, his fingers exploring and seeking and then finally cupping my bare flesh. I shudder and twist away. He instantly releases me and, for a Judas-moment, I would have willingly denied the love I feel for Fran to be back in his arms. He turns away from me, but not before I have seen the contempt in his eyes and in the dismissive shrug of his shoulders.

As I run from the room, I knock into a chair and fumble in frustration with the door. Eventually it opens, rucking up the carpet, leaving me scarcely enough space to edge into the welcoming darkness of the hall. I stand there, pulling at my clothes with ineffectual movements before groping my way towards the stairs. In bed, the sheets are cold. I lie there, trembling at the rag-bag disorder of my thoughts as I imagine the comfort of a body next to me, the stroking hands and my limbs responding, in the familiar pattern of shared nights. Fran appears and disappears in this kaleidoscope. I drift, miserably, into dawn-sleep.

I awake to a clear morning and stay there for a while without moving. Impulsively, I get up and pack my cases, with careless disregard for order, feeling nervous as I picture Fran's reaction. Downstairs, I try to eat breakfast, knowing that she is gazing at me in concern. Today is Saturday, and I hear Simon sawing at a branch in the nearby orchard. Later, I follow Fran when she goes to make the beds. I speak quickly and too loudly.

"It's been wonderful here, but I've been thinking about the work I have to catch up with. Perhaps I should leave today, although I hate to go."

Fran doesn't ask questions. She sits on the patchwork quilt, the line of her straight shoulders looking immensely vulnerable, her hands lying quiescent in her lap. After an interminable second, she raises her head.

"Rosemary, how I shall miss you. I understand though; I really do."

I move to her and we hold each other. I feel quite overwhelmed by her strength and love. Yet, last night, I could so easily have betrayed her. When we go downstairs, the boys refuse to accept my explanations.

"You mustn't go yet. You mustn't!"

In the end, Fran promises them a ride to the station. Soon the cases are in the Land-Rover. Fran has already told Simon that I am returning to London and from the end of the garden he waves, pointing to a half-sawn branch, indicating that it would be dangerous to abandon it. Looking back, I notice that he doesn't even turn to watch us depart. Fran's hair is escaping in tendrils from the knot on her head. She is wearing a tight tweed skirt and I feel strangely worried to see how this emphasises her long, skinny legs. Her eyes follow mine, as she carefully manoeuvres the car out of the driveway.

"I've always envied you, Rosemary. When I was about fourteen, I massaged my calves every day. Your breasts were larger, too! At times, I hated you."

I hunch my shoulders and stare straight ahead. I want to say that she should still hate me, but she is still talking.

"Anyway, Simon seems to have accepted that I'll never be buxom!"

We drive down the lane towards the main road. Over the hedgetops, I get my last glimpse of paint-bright colours on the sunny perimeters of the woods. I speak carefully.

"Are you ever jealous because of him?" "Yes. Very." "With reason?" "Plenty—for some years now." "What happens?"

I wonder why I am so persistent in my questioning.

"I take over the spare room for a month when things get bad."

Fran pulls up at the crossroads. We sense the children night be listening at the back, although as usual they have been arguing between themselves.

"Anyway," Fran continues, heading the car into town, "after a time, I went teaching again, when our youngest started school. It seemed strange, at first, but it's helped a lot. Maybe I shouldn't have married at eighteen. I had three children in as many years. I must be certifiable!"

Then we stop at the first set of traffic lights, and she turns to me for a moment. I notice her thick, dark lashes. She has many lovely features which are not immediately apparent.

"Simon's got some growing up to do, I'm afraid." She sounds vaguely apologetic. "Some people take longer than others."

Recognizing myself in the description, I say, "Amen to that!"

Our passengers lean forward.

"Is Daddy still growing?"

"His head is getting bigger all the time!" says Fran. The children laugh, falling around the seat in exaggerated attitudes. I realise she knows why I am leaving so suddenly.

Yet there are no reproaches on that composed face as she says, for the second time,

"How I shall miss you, Rosemary."

Hugging my elbows, I ask her:

"What must you think of me? I was ready for an involvement. I was stupid and mixed-up. I had to work out my life, and I couldn't think where to start."

Her eyes are on the road. "Don't say any more, Rosemary. Don't spoil what we share. Things will be fine for you now. I'm certain of it."

In awe of her maturity, I stare at this woman who is hardly a year older than I am. We look alike. We talk alike. But there it ends.

"Are you happier than you were, Rosemary?"

I search for words.

"I'm not sure, but what I do know is that seeing you has really helped."

She nods and says: "Good."

She grips the wheel firmly and stares straight ahead as she turns into the station approach. Again, she says: "Good."

She stops rather jerkily outside the entrance and smiles across at me, her friendship plainly visible. In a surge of tenderness, I long to return to the farm, to sit and talk in the haven of her living-room. The boys rush up and down, playing 'touch'. their cheeks flushed in the warm sunshine, while we stand by the steps feeling almost shy. We know we would break down if we embrace. Fran takes my hand and holds it against her face for a moment.

"I won't wait. I hate goodbyes."

The children are not so sensitive and throw their arms around me before racing off. Fran follows them, slowly, to the car, finally turning in her seat to wave. A breeze rustles the beeches as she drives away. When they are out of sight, I am still watching. Feeling suddenly chilled, I pick up my suitcase and move along the deserted platform dappled in slowly shifting patterns of bright sunlight.

Sauce For The Goose

First published 21st September 1985
Woman's Own

Abstractedly he says,

"You expect me to remember what kind of person I was when you first met me?"

He bends to the unit mirror to examine his face in close-up, turning sideways to study his chin-line as he knots his tie. He sees his wife in the king-size bed, her arms clasping her knees, the expression on her small face defiant but controlled. There is dignity in her anger.

"You know perfectly well what you were like, Phillip."

"No, I don't. It was nine years ago."

"Well, I'll tell you. You were a glutton for women. The only difference between then and now is that you're a slightly older glutton!"

He is vaguely shocked by her choice of words. He had married her because he had wanted a wife with such quiet composure. These days, she seems to take pleasure in disillusioning him.

"I was warned," she is saying. "Lots of people warned me."

"I'm surprised you managed to make it down the aisle, Gillian."

The unconcealed harshness doesn't escape her, and there is a sad little twist to her lower lip.

"I thought I could change you."

"Hah! The eternal conceit of women." He smooths his hair and reaches for his jacket. "Isn't it time you were getting up?"

"I don't have to be at the office until ten today." He stares at her, resentful that she can remain in bed on that raw morning.

She is wearing a creamy silk nightdress, layered with bands of fine lace, but he is oblivious to her elegance. Still sulking at her verbal attack, he asks:

"Where's my computer manual?"

"I've no idea."

"I'm sure I left it on this shelf. If Mrs Townsend has moved it . . ."

"She never touches your things. Ever since you were so rude to her."

He isn't listening. He finds the manual in a drawer. "Right. I'll be off, then." He pats his pockets, checking on his wallet, his keys.

"I want separate rooms, Phillip!"

He stops. "What did you say?"

She repeats the words, adding, "This time, I mean it."

Furious, he glances at his watch. "*Now* you tell me."

Even though she had guessed at his reaction, she feels hurt because he is not hurt. Not even slightly.

"Let's hear it then. What is it this time?"

His tone is deliberately patronising, provoking her with its underlying insolence. She makes herself look directly at him. He is still handsome and his stomach is flat, although a faint roll is beginning to show above his waistline. The well-tailored shirt is fractionally tight around the thick neck and shoulders. Once, she had delighted in that splendid body.

"I don't think I have to give you a reason, Phillip."

"If it's what I think you mean, my recent demands on you can hardly be classed as excessive."

"Lately, they haven't been."

Her eyes are cold enough to be above the barrel of a gun. "But when they're not, I always know why. That's what I can't accept any more. I refuse to be a part of your—your scheme of things."

He expels his breath in an exaggerated sigh.

"It's all in your mind, Gillian. You have no real cause to move out of our room!"

"The way I feel now, I'd like to move out of the house!"

"That's nasty, Gillian."

"I *feel* nasty!"

She swings her long legs over the side of the mattress and looks at him.

"Who is it this time? Kay Langdon?"

He is startled.

"What are you talking about?"

Knowing that he means 'How did you find out?' she shrugs and walks towards the shower-room door. With the stiffness of frequent rugger-playing, he is there before her.

"Whatever nonsense you've heard, I don't want you sullen and miserable when Harvey Newman comes to dinner tomorrow."

"Don't worry. Your Promotions Chief will be well catered for."

Her face is expressionless. She looks through him, speaking like a robot.

"The main course is already cooked and in the freezer. I shall remember the mints with the coffee. I shall wear my black chiffon."

He takes her seriously, smiles in relief while peering again at his watch.

"That's my girl. See you this evening then. I—er—may be late."

She remains rigid until she hears him going downstairs. Then, dry-eyed and empty, she starts on the pattern of her day.

In the corridors of Petersen's, where she is personal assistant to the junior partner, she is hailed by friendly voices she hardly hears. She stands in her office, her hands clenched, and bangs the copier in an effort to banish her tension. Mr Petersen emerges from his smoked-glass sanctum.

"I've been buzzing you, Gillian."

"We agreed I needn't come in until ten this morning."

She prepares to do battle with the weapon of her extra working hours the evening before, but he is immediately contrite.

"Of course. How stupid of me. I'll see you when you're ready."

He pauses, his Viking-blue eyes kind and inquiring. She sees the superb fit of his shirt, which isn't being strained by neck muscles. She had always been aware of his perfectly-cut blond hair and beard.

"Everything all right, Gillian?"

She smiles.

"Perfectly, thank you, Niels. I'll be with you in a moment."

For the rest of the morning, as if affected by a strange alertness, she is super-efficient.

"Perhaps being miserable makes you see things out of context, just as being ecstatic does," she says to Niels Petersen. "I feel I'm looking at everything from an entirely different viewpoint."

"So you are miserable, then, Gillian?"

"Oh, yes," she assures him. "Very."

He grins at her as he swivels in his desk chair. His voice is quiet, but the words are firm and clear.

"Then, why do you look so content, right at this moment, min elskede?"

Later, she rings her friend, Karen, in the Danish Embassy and asks her the meaning of 'min elskede'. When she replaces the receiver, there is a brightness in her face which had not been there before. She eats her lunch by the window of the office and watches the pigeons in the square below. The thrusting shoots of Spring are just visible in the railed gardens. 'I'd like to shut my eyes now and open them in May,' she thinks, throwing crumbs to the starlings. 'I want to opt out of bleakness and float downstream. Like Ophelia.'

When the Promotions Chief comes to dinner, Phillip gazes with approval at her metamorphosis into perfect hostess. Harvey Newman is the archetypal boss: silver-haired, silver-tongued and ruthless.

"Great little woman you have here, Phil," he beams, brushing cigar ash from his pale blue, broderie-anglais shirt front.

She fixes her expression and pours more coffee, mouthing appropriate replies at appropriate intervals.

"It will be mighty valuable for Phil to have the Boston experience next month," he is saying to her. "Totally different technique over there. He'll learn a lot in five weeks."

She freezes.

"Boston? Five weeks?"

"Pity you were tied up, dear lady. You'd have had a great time. Bit of sailing at Cape Cod, I shouldn't wonder. And a flight over to my place in Texas."

She longs to reply, 'But I'd love to come to Boston, Harvey. If I'd been asked!'

Instead she says,

"Oh, I'm sure Kay Langdon will benefit from the trip. I've heard that she's very ambitious." Her paper-thin words hang in the air.

Phillip chokes on his brandy, as Harvey Newman says,

"Yeah, Kay is really looking forward to it, I guess, but it surely is a shame you can't make it, Gillian. It surely is."

She allows her glance to settle slowly—very slowly—on her husband.

"Isn't it a shame, darling?"

She watches the acute embarrassment on his face. She smiles and smiles.

"Well," Harvey Newman is vaguely uneasy, sensing an undercurrent. "These things happen, of course."

"They do to me, Harvey. All the time!"

She continues to stare at Phillip. She continues to smile.

Later, in their bedroom, she asks Phillip for a divorce.

"No way," he says. "Out of the question."

"Why not?"

He has just emerged from the shower, still towelling himself. She watches him walk across the room and wonders how she was once attracted by the thick mat of hair on his chest. Wryly, she thinks, 'It came with the package! Along with the white teeth and the bold, black eyes.'

He drops the wet towel on the carpet, knowing how much it annoys her.

"Why not?" she repeats. "We've practically been divorced for the past year."

"Because it would affect my career at this stage. I need a wife."

"Like you'll need a wife on your trip to the States?"

"I meant for home entertaining. We'll have to throw quite a few parties when I'm Overseas Director."

He passes her chair as he prowls around the room. He doesn't even glance at her. Quietly, she asks him,

"So there will be trips abroad?"

He nods, standing by the bed, flexing his arms and shoulders. She feels repulsed as his rib-cage swells.

"Kay will handle those. After all, you do go out to work, Gillian. You haven't time for travelling."

Her voice remains cool and balanced.

"Is this home and away fixture list all arranged, then?"

He is pleased at what appears to be capitulation. "More or less. I'll give you plenty of warning. I'm so glad you're seeing reason, Gillian. We'll get along fine."

"But of course," she says. "I'm a great little woman, Phil, baby!"

She stands, beautiful in her soft negligee. He pulls back the duvet and pats the sheets, his eyes at last meeting hers.

"Come here. I want to make love to you."

She moves towards him. His arms reach for her. She picks up her book from the bedside table.

"I'm sleeping in the guest bed."

"Oh, no!" he mocks. "Not the guest bed again."

She pauses in the doorway.

"If you stop being a wife to me, I shall lose my love and respect for you," he informs her piously.

She closes her eyes.

"Did you say 'love' Philip? 'Respect'?"

"I need you, Gill. I need you as a person. As a friend." He makes a further effort.

"It would be hard to live without you."

She doesn't answer.

"Look," he coaxes her. "We could both do with a good holiday. Shall we go to the South of France sometime soon?

The bougainvillea will soon be out on the hills over Monte Carlo."

"Really?" she asks, with sudden interest. "I've often thought it must be lovely there. Surely, though, you're off to the States next month?" Confident now, his reply is instant. He had forgotten how worth while it was to be charming to her.

"Yes, but when I get back, we could go to France straight away, if you can arrange it."

He grins. Give her the vague promise of a holiday, and she'd be back in his bed in no time. It's too easy!

The white houses, in wedding-cake terraces, sweep down to the harbour.

"I hadn't realised how startling it would be," she tells him. "The sheer intensity of colour."

They stand together by the hotel pool, their bodies golden. They dive together, seal-like, barely fracturing the surface. They emerge to lie together, caressed by a satin wind. Above them, the bougainvillea brushes her bare shoulders. He pulls the petals and rubs them against her skin, bending to kiss the purple stain.

"I love you, Gillian. I need you as a person. As a friend."

She reaches to touch his face.

"Funny," she murmurs, admiring the Viking-blue eyes and the blond beard, so close to her now, "but I've heard those words somewhere before, 'min elskede'."

Possession

First published 1986

They have the beach to themselves.

"I love the sea in winter," she is saying.

She shifts her body on the driftwood log, leaning on her knees as she watches the waves become ruffles over the shallows to dissolve into green-marbled foam. A while ago, they had raced along the shoreline: he, with his long stride, easily beating her. He is caressing her shoulder, making ever widening circles until, still gentle, his hand explores beneath her scarf and works upwards to her earlobe. She looks across at him.

"I could stay here forever. Do we have to go back today?"

Almost immediately, he withdraws his hand. His sigh is so slight it could be an expulsion of breath.

"You know why, Val. Try rephrasing the question."

She wrinkles her nose at him.

"When will I see you again?"

"On the twenty-sixth of March."

She lowers her gaze, glad that her long hair is curtaining her face.

"It's in your diary already, isn't it? Crammed in between your other appointments."

"Now, now. Travelling is part of my job, you know that."

He reaches to twist her hair into yellow strands.

"I want to be with you Tom, in your flat."

"I've told you that will happen. I've asked Paula to leave."

"Tell me again."

"She'll be leaving as soon as she finds somewhere else."

As always, she feels vaguely sorry for this girl who has shared his life for the past two years.

"What did she say?"

He stretches his legs, the heels of his boots making rounded hollows in the cold damp sand.

"Well, what would she say, Val? She knew it wouldn't last."

She glances around, wondering what is responsible for the sudden chill that permeates her padded jacket. She looks sidelong at the strong thighs and broad shoulders, then bends towards him, trailing a piece of marram grass across his cheek.

"Not like us," she says. "We're different."

"Everyone's different. Each relationship is an entirely new experience."

"Is that all I am? Another experience?"

"You're too serious today, Val." He pulls his heavy oiled wool sweater from around his shoulders. "I thought we'd talked this through."

"It's just that . . . well, I've known you for five months, and she's still living with you."

He is pulling the sweater over his head. A part of her mind detaches itself as she watches his actions.

"Did you know it's always head first and arms afterwards for men?" she says. "Women are just the opposite. There must be a reason for that."

"You've been seeing too much of Robert the psychologist," he scoffs at her. "There's nothing Freudian about putting on a sweater. It simply means that women are fussy about their hair!"

On the drive back to London, she is quiet. He doesn't seem to notice. He switches on the car radio, his fingers waving in time to the beat against the steering wheel. When they reach the street of suburban houses, where her flatlet is one of many, he leans across to kiss her.

"The twenty-sixth then," he says. "Where shall we go?"

"I really don't mind. Anywhere," she tells him, knowing that she means 'anywhere with you'.

Amused, he touches her cheek.

"That's my girl."

When he drives away, she remains standing in the dark long after he has gone, feeling a disgust for her eagerness in accepting whatever he offers simply to be certain of seeing him again. She was successful, with her career in public relations. She should have assurance and confidence with men. Perhaps she should ask Robert to analyse her and tell her why she had two broken engagements. She smiles as she thinks of Robert. There is a man, safe and reliable, who would always care for her. With him, there would be no nerve-racking experiences when the sum and substance of her days seemed poised on a razor's edge. Within the week, she rings Tom's business number. An impersonal voice informs her he is in Rome for a conference.

"When will he be back, please?" she asks, her voice paper-thin.

"On the twenty-fifth, late in the evening. Who's speaking? Can I take a message?"

"It doesn't matter."

She replaces the receiver guilty because she has suspected him, yet happy and relieved that he told her the truth.

One Sunday afternoon, she and Robert walk across the park, where the weak Spring sun is trying to warm the branches of the trees. She has noticed, lately, how her perception has become alive to symmetry and contours.

"It's a kind of awareness which has built up over the last few months," she tells Robert, unconscious of the expression on his face. "Is it because I am happy?"

"I doubt it. Sometimes you've been downright miserable." He is faintly cynical, but today he is also abstracted.

Sensing his vagueness, she asks: "Is anything wrong?"

He glances at her. She sees the strength and kindness in his long-boned features and the way his tight-curled hair is so well cut, it seems stitched to his head, saying again: "Anything wrong?"

"No."

"What then?"

"I'm leaving London."

"You *can't* Robert!" she protests. "*Why?* Please don't walk so fast, I can't keep up with you."

They have almost reached Kensington, and he slows down.

"Because I am starting a practice in Herefordshire. That's one reason. The other, you must work out for yourself."

"Is Tom the problem?"

"Only to you."

Still hurt at the thought of existence without him, she is defiant.

"I've always been honest with you about Tom. Anyway, I know exactly how I feel and what I'm doing."

"Do you?" A shadow of a grin touches his mouth. "To understand oneself is the classic form of consolation. To delude oneself is the romantic."

"Stop psychoanalysing me!"

"Well, you're not a realist, are you, Val? Worse than that, perhaps, you want total control of the men in your life."

They have reached the road where Robert turns off. For a moment his fingers stay on her shoulder as he kisses her.

"Possession isn't love, Val."

Abruptly, he leaves her. Frightened suddenly, she calls:

"Let me know when you move. Will I see you again?"

"That's entirely up to you, love."

He doesn't turn his head as he walks away. She stands, forlorn, the chill air making her shiver.

On the twenty-sixth, when Tom phones her, she says:

"It's such a lovely day. Shall we drive into the country?"
"I've a better idea. We'll have a meal somewhere, and then you can come back to my flat."

"But what about Paula?"

"She'll be away for the weekend. Her mother's not well."

She is excited. Her relationship with Tom has always been marred by the fear of interruption. Somehow, it has outraged the delicacy of emotion she wants in their loving and she feels sure that, safe in his home, she might even find a sense of belonging. After their meal, they stroll towards the flat in Earl's Court. Lying with him in the big double bed, their unhurried love-making has the quality of perfection, leaving her warm and triumphant. The curtains are open to the moonlight, and she stares at the frieze of plaster roses on the corniced ceiling.

"I love old houses, Tom."

He leans across her, with touching fingers, his eyes dark and lazy.

"The moon's turned you to marble. And here—and here—are shadows."

Contented, she kisses him, repeating, "I love old houses."

Yawning, he falls back on his pillow. "Why?"

"Oh, the daytime silences. The night-time stirrings. Do you want to hear what else?"

He shifts to his side, facing her. "No. But I'm sure you'll tell me."

"The blowing trees, and the walled garden, full of secrets, where children can play."

He yawns again. "You're starting to sound domestic. Turn your back to me, Val. We'll sleep like spoons, my lovely."

She stays awake, her mind a kaleidoscope of dreams, while beside her, his arm heavy around her waist, Tom's breathing becomes deep and regular. Within the next six weeks, Tom goes to Paris. He goes to Boston. At the beginning of May, he snaps:

"I really will give Paula an ultimatum soon. Don't keep on, Val."

He goes to Budapest.

Angry and bewildered, she visits his flat. The girl who answers her knock has thin, pale features and a composure reflected in the elegance of her long, trousered legs and silk shirt.

"Yes, I'm Paula." The brown eyes are quizzical but not unfriendly. "You'd better come in."

Inside the flat, Val looks away from the open door of the bedroom. Paula brings coffee.

"I'm sorry Tom's not back, yet," she is saying. "He isn't due from Budapest until tomorrow." She puts the tray on a low table. "Have you known him long?"

"Quite a while. We're good friends." Val pauses. "We're also lovers."

Paula's face is expressionless. Picking up her cup, she moves to a hard backed chair, her head on one side in quiet appraisal.

"Tell me, why are you here?"

"To make you see how wrong you are to keep us apart."

"To keep you apart?"

Val gains courage from the soft voice.

"By staying on when he wants you to leave."

"I see."

Paula sits, very straight. Staring at her, Val wonders if she has imagined a faint pity in the kind eyes.

"Is that what he's told you, Val?"

"I do believe him, you know."

"Yes, I'm sure you do. I hope you will also believe me, when I say he has never once asked me to leave. You see, Tom likes things the way they are, because he's scared of being taken over."

"He asked me back here one night, two months ago, when you were visiting your mother."

Paula shrugs. "That was to keep you happy. It's possible you were pressuring him a bit?"

Val thinks of her insistence on sharing his life. She remembers his lack of response when she enthused about old houses. 'You want total control of the men in your life,' she hears Robert saying. She pushes her thoughts away.

"Of course I wasn't pressuring him."

Her clenched fingers emphasise the small bones on the backs of her hands.

"Tell me, why are you living here with him, if he prefers to live alone?"

"Tom knows I don't want permanency, at least not yet. Neither, I'm certain, does he. My first marriage was a disaster."

Paula leans forward. "We have a perfect understanding. No demands. No commitments."

There is a dignity in the tilt of Val's chin.

"You could be saying these things so that you can keep him for yourself. What makes you think I am not the right one for him? I've had enough experience to realise I love him."

"Possession isn't love, Val."

Again, that irritatingly knowing voice . . .

"You may love him, but would you ever trust him?"

"He'll change for me."

Paula hesitates, her nails tapping on her cup.

"Look, Val, there's something I feel you should know. He didn't stay on his own in Paris. Or in Boston. And he isn't alone in Budapest. There is a girl in his office who is only too willing to travel, and when he's tired of her, there will be others. That's the way he is."

Val has jumped to her feet and is reaching for her shoulder bag. Paula starts to get up from her chair, but changes her mind, her face troubled.

"Maybe you could be the one to curb him, Val. Perhaps I'm wrong."

Val stands quite still. The conciliatory words trigger an emotion that she does not recognise as a sense of release, a new beginning.

"No, Paula," she says. "I don't believe you're wrong at all."

Slowly she moves, willing herself to walk with purpose, across the room and down the stairs, and out of the hall door. Outside in the dusky street, there will be time to think.

Cry for Joy

1987

Because he is silent, I, too, am silent. Yet this barrier between us, he swears emanates from me. We chip at our emotions, within the emptiness of these confining walls.

For friends, we wear our cheerful masks, the ones with upturned mouths. We talk of children politics and issues of the day while ignoring cars or costs or holidays. Snow-mountain mornings and seaside afternoons are memories for a while. Eight months earlier, I had consoled David when he was made redundant.

"We needn't go away this year, and we'll forget about putting in a new kitchen. I don't mind." I was generous in my new-found martyrdom. "It's only temporary."

After the initial blow to his thirty-four years old pride, he also had bounded high. That's the way when you fall flat on your back. He had glanced around our comfortable living-room and I knew he was assessing the things we had worked for to make a home for the four of us. I saw his eyes linger on the hired video.

"That can be the first to go," I had told him. "I even found the children taping the test card the other day. It's got ridiculous!"

David had reached out to me, his hands warm and strong. In those days, his confidence was only bruised, not shattered and he was still in command of himself. Still full of hope.

"Well, just for the time being, we can manage with the tatty kitchen and send the video back. But we'll have that holiday in France, Rachel. It'll be something to look forward to."

I had hugged him in our hour of optimism, feeling almost proud of our sacrifices.

"Maybe you're right about the holiday, David, for the children's sake. Anyway, it isn't until September,"

"I'll have another job long before then," he'd said. "After all, I haven't been sacked. The form just went out of business, that's all."

"Which is why your redundancy is next to nothing. It would've helped so much to have a lump sum."

I hadn't meant to remind him of that and I wasn't surprised at the sharpness of his reply.

"What's happened has happened Rachel, and we mustn't think of maybe. Now is now."

But 'now' is discovering how even an experienced advertising man is simply another statistic in the job-queue quicksand. 'Now' is my helplessness seeing someone so young become so bitter. We discuss whether or not to sell our house.

"People are prepared to pay over the odds to live here," says David, watching my expression. "We could buy a cheaper place on the new estate."

Through the window, I see our village green with its cottages and duckpond. We were so lucky to find this house in the first place—the chance would never come again. Besides, the children have grown up here. And I have a part-time job in the local bank. I say the only thing I can think of.

"Not our home—not unless things get desperate."

I see the relief on his face and I know I have given him the answer he wants to hear.

"You'll find another job," I assure him. "It's a question of being patient, that's all."

Our children are slowly realising what their father's unemployment means to them. I eventually have to say, "I'm afraid we won't be going to France on holiday after all."

They are apprehensive and, because they are aware that their response is selfish, they become resourceful.

"Liz's parents have booked for France at the same time as we were supposed to be going," says Laura.

I look at my nine-year old daughter, knowing that she has put words into my mouth.

"Perhaps you could go with them? I'll ask." I smile to show her I was aware of being manipulated. "Liz would probably be glad to have a friend to go with."

Then I hear my son's voice.

"There's a scouts' camping trip to Cornwall in September, Mum," Tim says. "The same two weeks so . . . maybe—"

"All right. All right." I sound peevish. "I expect we might be able to manage that. We'll see."

I am resentful of them and of the independence that can seemingly rise above acceptance. I am sure they care, but I begrudge them their ability to adapt for their own immediate benefit. I had also adapted to start with, to keep us afloat. But these are thistledown days. David is becoming tense and irritable with so many rejections without even an interview. Needing the warmth of each other, as well as the passion, we lose them both from near-apathy.

"It's no good," groans David, falling back on his pillow. "I didn't know it did this to you. I can't even love you, Rachel."

I reach out to him. "Don't worry. You're tired."

"Tired!" he explodes. "How can I be tired? I just write letters all day long."

I look at him. I cannot tell him how he's changed, or how the worry-lines are newly-formed.

"You're good at your job. Someone'll have the sense to realise that soon."

"Will they?" I cannot remember such dreariness in his voice. "Some hopes!"

We have now cut out anything that might be termed even a small luxury, and I have taken on as many extra hours as the bank can give me. David's small redundancy payment has long ago vanished, while always with us are our fears for the future. I refuse to break down in front of the family, for crying is a private thing, unless you cry for joy. Also I still have hope, where David's has dwindled, so I decide to fly a flag in this puffball existence.

"You WHAT!"

David bangs his fist on the table, scattering cornflakes from his cereal bowl. I look away from his angry eyes, but I remain defiant.

"I've booked a two-roomed cottage on Skye," I repeat. "I've been saving something each week from my job, and we go by coach and boat, so we don't need a car." I hesitate for a moment, before I add, "I've arranged it for when the children are away, so it can be just the two of us. We need a holiday."

He stares at me, his anger abating. Then he leans across to take my hand, lowering his head to rest against it, his hair soft on my fingers. I look down at him, seeing streaks of grey in the dark curls which have not been there before.

"Oh, David, David," I say, with a love and compassion as deep as I have ever felt, while we stay there, together, drawing comfort from each other.

I wake one morning. He stands before me with a loaded tray, a letter in his hand.

"Breakfast in bed, darling," he says, smiling and quiet, "to celebrate."

I pull myself up against the pillows, as he carefully sets the tray on the bedside table. I see steaming coffee, pale yellow triangles of toast, a soft-boiled egg. And a single rose. He flourishes the typewritten page.

"Accepted," he reads. "Out of forty-six candidates. Start in October."

I hold out my arms. Our embrace is warm and sweet and thankful, before he moves slowly away from me.

Joyfully, I see us in our end-of-summer cottage, with gulls on the roof and heather on the hills.

He is laughing as he waves the letter.

I am crying as I smell my rose.

Hold a Candle to the Sun

Because he is silent, I, too, am silent.
Yet, this dreariness, he swears, emanates from me.

We chip at our emotions. Eroding, never shaping,
Within this emptiness of four, confining walls.
For strangers, we don our cheerful masks. The ones
With upturned mouths. We talk of children, politics,
And issues of the day. And of pipe-dream holidays.
Snow-mountain mornings and dog-day afternoons
Are memories which may never be renewed.

But now is now, and we cannot think of maybe.
Tomorrow becomes today. Today stands still.
Now is stretching from the dole-queue quicksand.
Now is weeping. A private thing unless you weep for joy.
Now is helplessness to see a man so shrewd become so aged.
His loss of dignity negating life, making him mindless.
Needing his comfort as much as he needs yours,
You pray he will be recognised again.

And when he asks; 'Am I too old?'
You cannot tell him how he's changed,
Or how the wrinkles on his face are newly-formed.
Thistledown days. Diminishing days. Standards are one thing,
Keeping them, another. Wanting the warmth of each other
Without the passion. We lose them both for want of trying.

To cross the bridge between redundancy and hope
Is to hold a lighted candle to the sun.

I wake one morning. He stands before me with a loaded tray,
A letter in his hands. 'Breakfast in bed,' he says,
Smiling and quiet, 'to celebrate this day.' A pot of coffee,
Pale yellow triangles of toast, a soft boiled egg.
Marmalade in china jar, with silver spoon. A single rose.
He is laughing as he waves the letter.
I am crying as I smell my rose.

Kathy's Kingdom

First published 6th February 1988
Woman's Weekly

Sitting in the bed, alert as a bird, she pushed her silky hair behind her ears. Her eyes were mysterious and pansy-dark. Her mouth was strong. With small, firm fingers she grasped her wrists across her nightgown and leaned, straight-backed, against her pillows glancing at the man beside her.

He stirred, half-raising his tousled head.

"Aren't you tired, Kathy?'

"Not a bit."

"Have you tried to sleep?"

"Well, no. I often sit up like this. I can feel this solid old house guarding us."

"I wish you'd settle down."

She didn't seem to notice his exaggerated sigh.

"It's such a lovely night," she said. "We were right to buy a house with high ceilings. Plaster roses were meant for moonlight."

Resignedly, he propped himself on one elbow as she turned to him.

"I want four children, Alex."

"No way," he told her. "Three are more than enough."

"Oh, you don't mean that. I know you don't."

He started to turn away, but she caught his hand. "Do you remember what you said to me a while ago?"

"Not really, Kathy."

"You said that I was beautiful."

Because he felt she required a response, he said:

"I meant it at the time."

But his tone was flat and his interest no match for hers.

91

She laughed. Drawing his hand away, he glanced at the bedside clock. Tiredly he told her;

"Now please go to sleep. I have to start early at the office tomorrow."

Her actions were precise as she flattened and smoothed her pillows. She patted him on the head and tucked the duvet around his neck. Keeping his back to her, he thought, 'we've been married ten years and I function well within my guide-lines. I am also manoeuvred and programmed and I could very well end up like a compressed square of metal in a used car dump'.

The next day at work he voiced his thoughts to Celia Jarvis without really meaning to. Celia had a way of encouraging such confidences by remaining silent at vital moments, her brows arched questioningly, her eyes diamond-bright. She leaned back in her chair, behind the impressive width of her desk. Her personal plaque said *Public Relations Consultant*.

"You've been married quite a while, haven't you Alex? Time for a firm stand. Kathy the perfectionist is obviously getting you down."

"She's a splendid wife," he said.

Celia smiled, showing her large, slightly wolfish teeth.

"With deeper connotations than the word itself implies?"

He hesitated. "She's a precision planner. A forward-thinker."

"I know, Alex. I know. I've been to your house, remember? I've seen the set-up. Everything neatly stacked. Decor, garden layout, furniture and children by permission of Kathy."

There was an almost imperceptible pause before she added, "Bless her!"

"She does a part-time job while Emma's at nursery school," he mused. "I don't know how she fits it all in, especially when the boys are at home."

"See what I mean?" said Celia. "She's the ultimate woman and you're conscience-stricken because you're rebelling against her."

He stared at the long, amused face. He knew she was right.

"She's a very good wife."

He was aware that he didn't sound convincing. "Great strength of character. Utterly competent."

"So was Delilah. And look what happened to Samson! Does Kathy cut your hair, by any chance?"

Alex coloured as he recalled Kathy saying, "I can do it just as well as that hairdresser you go to. Why don't you let me? I know what style would suit you."

He slammed the door of his office, with Celia's gravel-laugh ringing in his ears.

As he put the key in the front door, the familiar smell of red-bean casserole wafted from the kitchen. Kathy was fond of casseroles. They were ordered and self-contained. She liked neat roasts and plump little chickens. She didn't like mixed grills. He stood in the cool of the sitting-room, watching his family through the open French windows. The lawn was impeccably mowed, the edges razor-cut. The borders were massed with pinks and blues, because Kathy disliked oranges and yellows. He remembered saying, "But I want sunflowers."

She had stopped to make a wrinkly face at him, then continued to plant her delphiniums. There was a pool, just centre-left of the rockery, and a sand-pit for Emma in an appropriate corner. Everything was discreetly spaced. Everything was right. He closed his eyes, hearing Celia's drawling voice. Determinedly, he stepped out onto the terrace.

"I don't like casseroles," he announced loudly.

The children looked round at him and waved. Kathy came over and linked his arm.

"I'd prefer a mixed grill for a change," he told her.

Her smile was vague.

"Come and see the patch I've been digging, I thought we'd grow herbs."

He glanced at the flower-beds as she led him to the end of the garden.

"I want marigolds," he said, "and nasturtiums. Sun-colours."

"We could have thyme and rosemary here." Kathy was indicating her freshly-dug earth.

He gave her another chance, speaking slowly and deliberately.

"How about a summer-house? It could double for a workshop or a games-room."

"It really wouldn't look right, Alex."

She wasn't even looking at him, as she bent to smooth the soil.

"Now hurry up and get changed. You can mix some drinks while I finish the cooking."

"Kathy!"

He realised that his voice was a near-shout.

"Will you listen to me? Can I have a thinking reply for once?"

She looked up in surprise.

"Whatever do you mean?"

For a moment, he stared at her, his anger turning to emptiness.

"Never mind."

Abruptly, he left her and walked back to the house, passing his sons as they fought for the swing which hung, well hidden from the house, on a chestnut bough. He transversed the stepping-stones across the weed-free grass, his heightened awareness making him acutely conscious of the blues and mauves of the delphinium bed. 'For ten years I've been her consort,' he thought, 'and this is her kingdom!'

He strode through the tidy kitchen, pausing at the open door of the dining-room. The table was laid with precision. A candle stood, sleek as a rocket on its floral launching pad. He had a mad desire to mix up the cutlery and spill the salt, but he went, instead, to the Victorian mantelshelf and moved a vase from the left side to the right. Later, when Kathy was serving the casserole, she raised her head, frowning. Without comment, she walked across the room and returned the vase to its exact, original position.

Next day, Celia studied him, her eyes curious.

"I'm not sure if I can arrange for you to have the executive flat at such short notice, Alex. It's usually booked in advance."

His words were a command. "I want that key for tonight!"

She raised her eyebrows. "My! Aren't we masterful!" She placed her coral-tipped fingers on his sleeve. "Kicked over the traces at last, have we?"

"I need to think for a while," he said. "I feel that I must review things from a safe distance."

"Well," she purred, "isn't it lucky the company provides a flat for top management and that I'm here to pull some strings for you?"

He scowled at her. "I shall be working on the Thompson report," he told her, "as well as coming to terms with myself."

"Of course." She grinned.

His gaze travelled from her long, beautiful legs to her flame-coloured, corkscrew curls. Unblinkingly, she returned his scrutiny. He rang Kathy in the afternoon.

"I have to work a great deal of overtime on this new project for a few days. I'll be staying in the firm's flat."

"I see," she said in a small voice.

As she put down the receiver, he felt a surging disappointment that she hadn't protested at his absence.

When he came home three days later, she was collecting Emma from nursery school. He entered the house and realised it was the first time he had ever been there when it was empty. He was instantly desolate and sat like a nervous stranger on the edge of the settee, still holding his briefcase. The sound of a key and Emma's bright chatter roused him. Kathy walked into the room, her expression guarded.

"I saw the car," she said. "Have you been here long?"

"A while," he said.

She turned to Emma. "Go and play in the garden, sweetie. The boys will be home soon from school."

Her dark eyes were sober as she shut the door and faced him. Because he didn't know what to say to her, he asked her,

"Is something worrying you?"

"Am I like my mother, Alex? I want a truthful reply."

He blinked at her.

"Hardly! Your mother was bossy and interfering . . ." His voice trailed away before her impatient nod.

"See what I mean?"

"Yes, but she was absolutely unbearable," he protested.

"I may grow like her though. I've got some of her worst traits. Don't think it doesn't worry me." She folded her arms and crossed to the window. "I know I was getting on your nerves. I'm not insensitive."

"Insensitivity has never been one of your faults, Kathy. You were just holding the reins too tight, that's all. I think I had a bad reaction. I've been feeling a bit unsettled lately about all kinds of things."

He waved a hand to encompass everything and nothing. She was watching Emma swing on the garden gate, waiting for her brothers.

"I'm not sure if I can stop being a perfectionist, Alex."

He leaned forward, examining his locked fingers. He looked very young in his dark suit.

"I think you could try," he said slowly.

She had walked over to stand in front of him, her arms hugging her body, one hand sliding up and down her elbow.

"There are times," he said, "when I can't accept it at all. I seem to be fighting against a takeover." He paused, still studying his fingers. "In his own home, a man should feel like a man."

She perched on the opposite chair, sitting straight, facing him. She spoke slowly and carefully.

"We couldn't survive without you, Alex. So, if ever a man should feel like a man, you surely must."

Her words washed over him like a warm shower, but he didn't move. When she spoke again, her tone had a huskiness which at once alerted him. After ten years of marriage, he could recognize when Kathy felt insecure.

"When you were staying in the firm's flat was—was Celia with you?"

He looked up quickly, catching her emotions before she could turn away. In that brief moment, she was frightened and immensely vulnerable.

"No," he said, but he couldn't meet her eyes.

He rose awkwardly, mumbling that he was thirsty, and walked towards the kitchen door, glad of the respite. As he entered the room, he was dazzled at first by the afternoon sun. Then, slowly, his lips parted in disbelief. His eyes moved from the unwashed dishes on the draining-board to the total disorder of Emma's lunch on the table. The floor wasn't exactly dirty, but neither did it shine. The blind had been pulled up and allowed to sag, tiredly, at one corner. His final glance at a bowl of dried-up flowers made him gasp. Never had Kathy allowed her cut blooms to come anywhere near to dying, even with dignity!

"You see," she said quietly from behind him, "I went to pieces when you didn't come home. I just lost interest."

He fetched a drink from the refrigerator and she followed him back to the sitting-room. He sank into an armchair, still seeing the chaos of that bright kitchen. She came over to him to kneel in front of him and she spoke as if her thoughts were far away.

"I'd like a huge pine table for our five children, Alex."

"I don't want five children," he replied. "I might think about four."

"You shall sit at the head of that table, Alex darling!"

Because her words were sweet, his protest was mild. "Why do you plan so much?"

But he rather liked the picture of his family gathered in the lamplight. Playing her game, he chuckled,

"Perhaps I'll wear a gold watch-chain!"

"This house is our future," she told him earnestly. "Do you want to know why I love it?'

Gently he tugged her hair.

"No, but you'll tell me Kathy."

"I love the daytime stillness and the night time stirrings. And the whispering trees when I'm hanging out the washing. And the stained glass, throwing blue and amber squares on our tiled hall."

Speaking quickly, as if to get the words out before she regretted them, she added, "I'd grown tense, and I didn't realise it. Even the slightest thing out of place worried me. I think I was becoming neurotic."

He felt no triumph. Only an emotion which he knew was pure compassion for this small, intense figure with her head against his knees.

"You do too much, Kathy. We'll get help in the house. You must learn to delegate."

Irrelevantly, she asked him, "Do you remember my grandmother?"

"Only vaguely," he said.

"When she was ninety-four, she used to plant seeds in little boxes on her window-sills, because they represented another year of life."

He was curious. "Why did you tell me that?"

"I don't know," she said. "Perhaps it seemed to fit in with the things which have a meaning for me."

She took both his hands in hers, touching them with her soft cheek. He drew her towards him, knowing that she had neatly put his worries into perspective. Like her mother's mother, she planted her seeds for tomorrow, because she believed in herself and in her family. Just as she believed without question that he hadn't spent a night with Celia. As he bent to kiss her, he heard the boys and Emma running up the garden path, squabbling and pushing to be first in the door.

He was glad to be home.

An Intelligent Girl

First published 1989
Woman Summer Special

Mike's flat-topped desk was striped in sunlight. I could hear the muted roar of city traffic in that quiet room where it was always possible to turn my mind from high pressure to a gentle simmer. I'd been explaining about Rob, a recent addition to our sales staff.

"It was instant attraction," I said.

Mike grunted. "If that's your type. Good at his job, is he?"

"Ambitious to a fault," I assured him.

Mike half turned from me on his swivel chair, reaching for a pile of documents.

"He'd be out on his ear, if he wasn't. J.D. would see to that."

"It's been a long while since I felt like this," I told him. "I don't get much time for emotional workouts. J.D. keeps me hard at it."

"And rightly so." Mike spoke with mock severity. "Seriously, though, an involvement for you usually means total commitment. Just be careful, Chrissie. Don't play your aces."

I coloured at his accuracy. I am as intense about my relationships as I am about my career. Although I have the sense to keep the two apart, I invariably peak quickly and stay on a high. That's fine, when I am a decision maker for J.D., but dangerous when I meet a charmer like Rob.

"Thanks for listening, Mike." I really meant it.

His face was expressionless as he picked up his dictaphone.

"Take care," he repeated.

Mike was in advertising. He'd gone out of his way to help me when I'd joined the company and within eight months I'd become personal assistant to the junior director, John Dalby. Mike had been the first to congratulate me, with a bunch of freesias on a table in my new office.

"They were selling them off cheap," he'd said.

When I'd met Rob a few weeks ago I knew he'd been having a liaison with Poppy, our public relations consultant, who had known him before he started with us. Poppy had hair the colour of her name and a physique like a warrior queen. She was also unscrupulous and incredibly shrewd. Over a drink at the local after work, Rob had manoeuvred me away from the others.

"You have remarkable eyes," he told me.

"Like limpid pools, are they?"

I rubbed my finger round the rim of my glass, trying to keep things on a light-hearted level, until I got my bearings with this man. He had moved closer.

"Dark and unfathomable, I'd call them."

"Like treacle?" In that moment of laughter, I had noted how extremely nice looking he was. Good teeth and a well proportioned body, with no hint of fat. In contrast, I hardly reached to his shoulder because I'm quite short, with black hair, which I've been told is exceptionally glossy, and a tilted nose. I walk briskly, with turned out feet, especially when I'm happy. I was aware of far more than physical attraction to this man. Despite his confidence, he had a lost-boy look, as if he had never found what he was searching for. It was irresistibly appealing and I had decided, there and then, that Poppy needed some competition.

"Chrissie," said a sarcastic voice. "Was there anything else?"

I'd been half sitting on Mike's desk. I jumped up and opened the file I'd been carrying.

"Sorry. I was deep in thought. I like to allow myself several periods of contemplation each day. It's a kind of renewal!"

"Well, go and renew somewhere else, will you?" he said sweetly. "I'm extremely busy."

I smiled at him. "I feel so relaxed in your room. There's no chance of any reveries upstairs when J.D.'s around."

The eyes behind the dark rimmed glasses studied me.

"If I didn't know that J.D. selects only the best for his personal staff . . ." he murmured.

With a reverence which I have never quite been able to lose, I indicated the top floor office suite.

"I *am* the best when I'm up there, believe me!"

I drew myself up to my full height, handing over the layouts I'd brought downstairs with me.

"I can assure you I'm high powered, competent and indispensable."

Mike raised his eyebrows.

"So. You wear different hats. Why do I have to see the one with 'I'm a dumbo!' written on the front all the time?"

"I shall use my influence with J.D. to get you fired," I threatened, as I left the room.

"Promises, promises," he mocked. "With a workload like this, I should be so lucky."

I walked briskly along the corridor, happily turning out my feet. Rob emerged from the lift and was suddenly right in front of me.

"I've been looking for you, Chrissie," he said. "Could you fit in a meal after work?"

I thought of the sliced liver in my fridge.

"Yes, please," I said.

He smiled down at me. "Make it as early as you can, then."

Two hours later, when I glanced at my watch, John Dalby asked, "In a hurry?"

"I'm going out for a meal with someone this evening, J.D."

He stretched. "Are we on schedule?"

"More than," I told him.

He stared at me as he stood up. He had rather penetrating eyes. His tallness blocked the light from the window as he eased his jacket over his shoulders.

"Have a nice time," he said.

In the restaurant, I said to Rob: "I thought you and Poppy . . .?"

"We haven't been out together for ages, Chrissie. We aren't really compatible."

I recalled Poppy in the wash-room, enthusing about Rob to another girl.

"Does she know that?" I asked.

"I think so," he said casually. "Poppy's been around."

We walked home under a summer moon. I wondered if Rob would ask to come into my flat, or if I should invite him in. As we approached the steps, he stopped and said, "We'll do this again."

I wanted to say 'When?' But I knew that wasn't the way to hold men like Rob. It's better to smile and say: 'Of course. It's been great.'

"It's been absolutely great," I told him. "See you at the office tomorrow."

I'd learned quite a lot since Mike had said to me once, "For an intelligent girl, you seem uncertain about men, Chrissie."

I had been indignant.

"At least I have only had two boyfriends. Look at all the females you've been out with!"

I met Rob several times in the next month. He was beginning to be insistent about our relationship. I tried to explain:

"I'm not ready yet, Rob. For me, it has to be the right place at the right moment. It has to be romantic."

He sulked a little, looking like a small boy, who had been refused an ice cream.

The following week, he said on the phone, "I've something to ask you."

Over the Steak Diane at our favourite eating place, he seemed so pleasantly excited that I was immediately responsive.

"I'm being sent to Florence for two weeks, Chrissie, and I wondered if you'd like to come too."

"You need a personal assistant?" I asked, surprised.

He was faintly sardonic.

"Not exactly." He leaned back in his chair, drumming the table with his fingertips. "I leave that to the J.D.s of this world."

I flushed. "Oh. You mean . . .?"

He nodded. "That's exactly what I mean! Have you ever been to Florence?"

I wanted to say that Florence was where I'd always wanted to go. And I thought of the Tuscany hills and the brown mysterious Arno.

"Chrissie?"

"The statue of David," I murmured. "The Ponte Vecchio."

"Are you due for a holiday?" There was a look of triumph on Rob's face. I paused, struggling to make dignity curb my enthusiasm.

"I'll let you know, Rob. I have to ask J.D." I said. "He may need me."

"Ah, Florence," said J.D. watching me closely. His eyes were alert. "This is rather a sudden decision, isn't it, Chrissie?"

To avoid his gaze, I asked, "Have you ever been there?"

"Elizabeth and I went in our student days, just before we were married."

I felt sad for him. "Talking about it must bring back memories."

"Maybe. I still miss her, of course, but she's been gone nearly five years, Chrissie. Time heals."

I had heard about the tragedy from Mike and, as I looked at J.D.'s strong face, I envisaged how one careless driver on a glassy December road had almost destroyed his life.

"Take more than a couple of weeks," he was saying. "You've done a splendid job with the Anderson contract. I couldn't have managed without you."

Still feeling vaguely depressed for him, I said, "Thanks, J.D." and left the room, closing the door with unusual gentleness.

Downstairs, I bumped into Poppy.

"I want to talk to you," she said.

Psychology is one of my A levels, so I know that if a female says she wants to talk to you, it doesn't usually mean she's dying to have a friendly conversation. Over a cup of tea in the canteen, I found myself making a defensive reply to her very pointed question.

"Rob's a free man, Poppy, and you haven't been out with him for ages, have you? But he shouldn't have been spreading it around that I'm going to Florence with him, before I've confirmed it."

"Which you're on your way to do now, I assume?"

She twisted a corkscrew curl in her tawny mane.

"Why?" I asked.

From the strange look in her eyes, I guessed that a crunch was imminent.

"Did you know he's married, Chrissie?"

"Married?" I repeated. "I'd heard he was divorced."

"This one is his second. She's an actress. She's very pretty."

She watched me, her green eyes speculative. I was trying to keep my voice calm.

"Were you aware of this when you went out with him?" I asked her.

She was completely at ease.

"Oh, yes," she said. "And I shall still go out with him if he asks me again. But I'm that kind of girl, Chrissie. You're not."

Rob didn't look secretive or ashamed at my question.

"I thought you knew. I would have told you if you'd asked."

"You expected me to go to Florence with you!"

"Don't blame me for inviting you. My marriage is having a bit of a rough ride at the moment and I'd have liked your company."

"I bet you would," I said bitterly. "To think I almost fell for it."

He was indignant, almost hurt. Then he smiled at me, his tone level and reasonable.

"You're an intelligent girl, Chrissie. No one was forcing you."

I walked down the corridor faster than I had ever walked before. Mike, coming from the other direction, paused outside his office.

"You're either unhappy or furious," he remarked, as I drew near.

"A lot of both," I told him. "How did you know?"

"Your feet aren't turning out."

I halted. "Can I come in for a minute, Mike?"

I flopped into a chair. "I'm finished with day dreaming," I said.

"It's over with Rob, is it?"

He crossed to the window and made a mock pistol shot at a mauve-breasted pigeon on the ledge outside. I could see a patch of pale sky above St Paul's and I swallowed a sob as I thought of the golden domes of Florence.

"I knew he was married. I also knew what your reaction would be when you found out."

"Supposing I hadn't?"

"Chrissie, you're a highly intelligent girl."

"I've heard those words before," I said. "Emotionally, I'm about as intelligent as a bowl of custard!"

He turned from the window.

"So, this is all part of your education. Rob's probably been good for you. Put it down to experience."

"Don't you dare say 'Life's rich tapestry!" I said.

He took off his glasses, replacing them almost immediately and ran his hand through his dark, curly hair. He sat on the corner of his desk staring at me.

"You must realise how I felt about you. How I've always felt about you, in fact."

I looked down at my fingers. They were tightly locked.

"I think I've known for a long time, Mike." Then, I lifted my head and said, slowly: "I was dreading when you might actually say it."

The silence seemed interminable as I watched Mike's shoe tap steadily against a chair leg. He stood up and went into his small washroom, where I heard him splashing water into a basin. When he returned, he was brisk and business-like. I wondered if he would shake my hand.

"Fine," he said. "Still good friends?"

He extended his big palm. We both laughed.

"One day, Chrissie, we'll remember this when we bump into each other in the street and I introduce my glamorous wife and fine sons."

I guessed at the depth of his hurt. "Oh, Mike, I'm sorry," I said.

For a moment we looked at each other and I thought of all the times he had given me strength and encouragement.

"Why don't I love you, Mike?" I asked, miserably. "When I like you more than any man I've ever met."

His kiss was not at all gentle, but it was obviously final.

"Chemistry," he said. "It happens all the time."

Five years later, on a trip to London, I returned to see them all. Rob's wife had run away with the producer of her latest play. He was now married to Poppy.

"I felt so sorry for him." said Poppy. "She even stowed the silver and china in cases marked HIS and HERS—mostly HERS, I might add—and she smashed his mother's wedding present fruit bowl!"

Mike proudly showed me a picture of his beautiful wife and two daughters.

"Fine sons!" I grinned.

"Well, who wants boys," he chuckled.

I sneaked another look at the picture with a surge of satisfaction. I noticed that his wife had black, glossy hair and dark eyes—like mine. He placed an arm around my shoulders and he and Rob, one on each side, walked me towards the swing doors.

"The company's never been the same, since J.D. was sent to Italy," said Mike.

"We've missed that man. He was dynamite," Rob added.

"He certainly was," I said.

I kissed them goodbye as they returned to the main office. I stood very still, my eyes following the two men who had assuredly influenced my life, and I was aware of an ache that was both sad and sweet.

"Are you ready, Chrissie?" said a deep voice.

Thankfully, I saw my husband smiling at me from the lift entrance.

I walked briskly down the passage towards him, turning out my feet.

"I'm ready, J.D.," I said.

May The Best Girl Win

First published 19th May 1990
My Weekly

It was at least a year before I could think of my mother without crying a little, and much longer than that before Kelso, my dad, stopped looking like a lost boy. Mum had related to Dad with a kind of awareness, which made her eyes soften and her hand stroke his arm, even while she murmured:

"Don't ever imagine you can fool me for one moment, Kelso Harvey!"

"Sweetheart," he'd say, "I'd never try!"

I believed him, and I was sure that she did too.

He didn't need to hide his popularity with women. He listened to their troubles and, although he was seldom lost for words, he knew when to say nothing. He must have married my mother at a very early age, because I'm eighteen and he's still in his thirties. He's a really attractive man, a bit like a young Michael Caine. It wasn't always sweetness and light, of course.

I was reading a book once in a corner of our warm kitchen, and Mum's rigid back, as she prepared a casserole, just about said it all. She shut the oven door, then turned to Dad, who was leaning against the wall with folded arms, his shrewd eyes attentive to her every word.

"It didn't take you two hours to walk that girl from your office to the station, Kelso."

"She missed her train, so I waited with her for the next one." His voice was calm. "She's just a despondent young woman from Accounts, with a mixed-up marriage. She needed help with her problems, love."

"You can find problems to solve within your own family, if you look for them," Mum said a little sharply.

He reached to take a creamy bud from a jug of roses on the window-sill, crossing the floor silently to place the bloom beside her on the worktop.

"She means nothing to me, Jeannie. You know that."

The stiffness left her, as her fingers tightened on the stem of the rose. There was a tilt to her chin, and her mouth went down at the corners, a sure sign that Mum had decided not to give in too easily.

"You don't get round me with a flower, Kelso, even if I do choose to believe you."

She walked past him, quite composed, and he watched her all the way to the door, with an expression on his face which I felt sure was admiration.

"Fair enough, sweetheart," he said. "Fair enough."

He spoke so softly that I almost fell from my chair in a sideways attempt to catch the words. I snatched up my book and held it level with my eyes, in a pretence of reading. Hearing his chuckle, I glanced up to see him gazing at me. His voice was lazy.

"Wouldn't it be easier, Miss Nosey, if you turned that book the right way up?"

Now, it's early summer, and I'm waiting to go to college in October. Dad has slowly been emerging from his grey void, where at first I could hardly ever reach him. This morning, as we sat together in the kitchen, drinking coffee, I heard at last the old jauntiness in his voice and saw the laughter in his eyes, and knew it was the start of a new way of life. I felt acceptance instead of sadness, as I thought of Mum, standing tall. Her arms were never empty. There was always shopping, or flowers from our garden, or someone's demanding kid held tight against her.

"We'll always miss her," I blurted out, "but life's got to go on, Dad, hasn't it?"

With a quick intake of breath he said: "It's hard to believe it's been nearly two years without her, Kate."

His fingers tightened around the steaming mug and I thought how strong his hands were, with their short fingers, and carefully trimmed nails—strong, yet sensitive.

I touched his arm, wanting to say something like: 'You always really loved her, didn't you?'

All I could manage was:

"You were always right together."

He looked across at me. "We understood each other. That's almost more important than loving."

"I'm over it, now. You're right, Kate, we have our lives to live. She would never have wanted us to go on grieving."

Impulsively, I told him, "I'm going to marry a man like you. He'll have a strong face and nice teeth and he'll belong to me."

He didn't immediately reply, but his eyes grew alert, and he stopped smiling.

"Belong? You're talking of total commitment, pet. Possession isn't love."

Surprised, I stared at him.

"It was a compliment," I protested.

He ignored me.

"Everyone needs a corner of their mind to themselves. Believe me, Kate, a man will respect you for knowing that."

"The boys I go out with aren't too bothered about respect," I muttered. "How will I ever learn to recognise these things?"

"It's a game of chance," Dad said.

He rose from the chair and studied me, his hands in his pockets. I noticed how the skin puckered around his blue eyes when he laughed.

"Don't worry, Kate. Being what you are, you'll narrow the odds. You've got a good head on your shoulders and you'll go for a meeting of minds. That will be important to you."

I'd have listened to anything he said at that moment, because it was the first time he had again become involved in my problems since Mum died, without a trace of sadness in his voice.

I spoke to Mrs McCluskie about our conversation and how Dad seemed at last to have come to terms with his life. Widowed Mrs McCluskie had been Mum's best friend for as many years as I can remember. When Mum died, she began to help out every morning with the housework and cooking. She disliked taking money for it, but as I got paid for my temporary job at the office where I was working until I started college, I insisted that she was equally entitled to a salary. She was a very private person. She rarely mentioned her twelve-year old son, who, I knew, had been causing her a great deal of worry ever since he was a small boy. I watched her, now, as she peeled potatoes with nervous energy, her back straight and rather tense, her dark curls bobbing fiercely as she moved.

"I'm glad for your father," she said in her soft voice. "It's not good to look inward for so long."

She dried her hands and sped across the kitchen on her winged feet to take something from the refrigerator. She was never one for chattering. Thoughts of college were ever present, ever exciting, but I worried more and more about my dad being alone when I left home. I decided to introduce him to Olivia, the golden-haired supervisor in our office. She came to supper and was a really good talker, but as soon as I realised she wasn't going to give anyone else a chance, I knew Dad would dislike her.

Naturally, she adored him. Everyone does. Well everyone except Mrs McCluskie, who never commented on him at all, unless I asked her.

"I know it was Mum who was your real friend," I said to her as we polished the furniture one day, "but you do like Dad, don't you?"

She didn't answer immediately, and her duster made smaller and smaller circles on the table until it finally stopped. She turned to look at me in a speculative kind of way, her slim body unusually still.

"Yes, I do," she replied. "He's a very likeable man. But if you expect to run his life, Kate, he'll react like a cornered animal. Jeannie knew exactly how to handle him."

"But Mum never gave in to him."

I remembered the proud lift of her chin and the turned-down corners of her full mouth.

"And he adored her, didn't he?"

Mrs McCluskie returned to her polishing.

"And he also respected her, Kate, because she never tried to dictate to him."

I thought of Dad saying 'possession isn't love'. Suddenly I knew what he meant.

I brought two other girls home from the office in quick succession to meet Dad. He would lounge about in check shirts and sweaters, looking more like Michael Caine than ever, his long legs getting in everyone's way. He was always polite and quite charming, but he remained as distant from them as the North Star. The last girl I invited seemed to attract him instantly. She was quiet and rather sweet, with a shy, almost frightened look about her.

Dad appeared to like talking to Mary, so I tactfully left them alone. They went out together a few times and I told Mrs McCluskie with pride that I'd managed to find a companion for him at last. Her only acknowledgement was:

"So you've fixed it, have you?"

There were two bright spots on her cheeks, as she moved briskly away from me.

"I'll want you to help me take down the curtains for dry-cleaning."

As we folded and labelled the curtains, I said to her: "How's your son? You never talk about him."

She looked across at me, and I somehow knew she was glad I had asked.

"Oh, Kate. I wish I knew what to do with him. He's always been defiant and stubborn, but he's getting worse, and it's a constant battle of wills. He needs a firmer hand than mine."

She allowed the curtains to slip to the floor. She seemed nervous and defenceless.

"I think I should also tell you that I might have to sell my house, unless I try for a full-time job," she went on. "But I don't want to leave here. It was Jeannie's home, and sometimes I feel she's still around."

It was the longest speech I had ever heard from Mrs McCluskie. Her eyes met mine, woman to woman. Warmth flowed between us and I felt older and wiser, not recognising my emotions, but wanting her to know I understood. We stayed there, together, for a long, shared moment, and I touched her shoulder, remembering how my mother had loved her. Then we picked up the curtains without a word and went on with the folding.

"Do you still see Mary?" I asked Dad that evening.

"No," he said lazily. "But she was a very nice girl. Why do you ask?"

"You were going out with her quite a bit at one time."

He leaned against the wall, his arms folded.

"She had a problem and I've been able to help her. That's all there was to it. I haven't seen her since."

I stared at him. "Are you sure?"

He looked surprised. "Of course I am. She had an ex-boyfriend who was trying to get money from her. He won't try again. Problem solved."

I didn't know that my chin had tilted and that my mouth had turned down until he said:

"Oh, Kate! You look so like your mother."

"Sometimes, I feel like her." I drew myself up. "But there are problems nearer home, Dad. Right here in this house, in fact. I'm talking about Fiona McCluskie."

"I hardly ever see her," Dad said. "She's usually gone home by the time I get back from work."

"Did you know her son's a little tearaway and that she's running out of money to pay her mortgage, unless she finds another job?"

He was startled. "I vaguely knew about her son, but not about the money. We'll have to offer her considerably more, Kate."

"She won't take it. She's known us for too long. She feels she's a part of us."

"She *is* a part of us." Dad wasn't leaning against the wall any more. His blue eyes were alert and serious.

"Fiona's always been a wonderful friend. She belongs here."

"Well, she's thinking of leaving," I told him. "And very soon."

"That's impossible. I must drive over to see her at once." He was already halfway to the door.

I didn't see much of my father for several weeks after that. We met, briefly, at meals, but he was often out in the evenings and at weekends, and I was busy with two part-time jobs trying to earn a little extra money for college.

I was happier than I had been for a long time—maybe because Dad was looking just like he did when he and Mum filled this house with their quarrelling and their love and laughter. One lovely, summery day Dad and Fiona stood in the shade of the birch tree in our garden while I photographed them with my new camera. Dad's arm tightened around her slender shoulders and he bent to drop a kiss on the top of her dark head, while he glanced thoughtfully at me.

"I think you had Fiona lined up for me all along, you young schemer," he said with a grin.

I pretended to study my camera. If that's what he believed, I might as well go along with it. He would never know that a moment of truth, when one woman confides in another, had given me the insight to wait for him to decide his own future—with just a little nudge from Daughter Kate! Importantly I said:

"Sometimes people set their eyes on far horizons and don't always see what's under their noses, Dad."

"It's you who were setting the horizons!" he protested. "Filling the house with your girl-friends!" I thought it better to change the subject.

"What's happening about your son?" I asked Fiona.

"Kelso will sort him out," she said. "He just needs a man to talk to him."

She smiled up at Dad with such total happiness that I felt almost jealous. He was watching me.

"Any more questions?"

I shook my head.

"Fiona's going to sell her house," he went on. "We felt that would be the best solution."

"Where will she go?"

"Where do you think, Kate?"

His blue gaze was quizzical. I had long ago accepted that he might not live alone, once he had emerged from his shadows. And I instinctively knew that my mother, with her warmth and wisdom, would have wanted Fiona McCluskie, above all women, to share his life.

Without quite knowing why, I was suddenly proud of being female.

"So you'll manage when I go to college?" I asked Dad. "You won't be lonely?"

I had expected him to reply, but it was Fiona who slipped her arm into his and looked across at me with that instant communication between us. Wisps of dark, cloudy hair fell softly around her ears and her expression was as mysterious as the Mona Lisa. She spoke directly to me, woman to woman. Her voice was quiet.

"No need to worry, Kate." With suppressed laughter, she added: "Problem solved."

The Same Mould

First published 1989
Woman Summer Special

They said it was impossible for me to be Julie's mother and that Julie herself, with her polished black hair and calm face, looked far too young to have a son of five.

"Of course, that accounts for it," they murmured, their eyes searching for furrows. "You'd had Julie at nineteen and she's done the same with Matthew. It's unfair, being a grandmother at thirty-eight!"

"I'd recommend it, though," I'd said, understating my exquisite awareness of the meaning of continuity, when I had first gazed down at Julie's son. Remembering how my daughter sees with my eyes, loves the things I love and is so much a part of me that we laugh or cry at the same time.

Today she comes to meet me at the gate. She is dressed to go out.

"Are you sure you can cope with Matthew for the whole day?" she asks.

"There's a good chance we shall bore each other to tears," I tell her, tripping over my grandson, who has crouched to study a beetle with that immediacy which doesn't involve a warning.

"If that happens," I continue, rubbing my ankle, "I'll exercise him in the park. Probably on a two foot lead!"

"You're a star," Julie says.

I smile at her. "Oh, I know!"

She looks so happy these days, and so relaxed, that it gives her an air of confidence she doesn't normally possess.

"Give my love to Sarah," I say. "I'm really pleased you've been able to see more of her lately."

"Borrowed time." Julie bends to hug her son. "Sarah usually lives out of suitcases. The price of being a film producer."

Together, we walk to the car. We are the same height, with the same long legs and narrow hips. Julie slides into the driver's seat.

"I'll be home well before Jonathan. He's going to a meeting."

She shuts the door and winds down the window.

"By the way, Matthew likes honey with his yogurt."

I raise my palms to the sky. "You think I don't know what Matthew likes? Now off you go."

For a moment Julie pauses, glancing across at the absorbed figure. Suddenly, and very quietly, she says:

"I don't like leaving him."

I bend to the window. "It's impossible for any woman to love her child twenty-four hours a day."

Julie's fleeting anxiety is replaced by a smile, as she waves and drives away. I look down at the small, sturdy boy, who is now standing up and working out the day's programme, with me no doubt, playing the exhausting role as his leading lady! I know from experience to get in first.

"You're too big to suck your thumb, mister!"

A glint appears in his eyes, but he continues to suck, while he gestures towards the garden.

"Football!" he commands.

"Not likely, my lad. I need a cup of coffee."

He studies me for a while, before accepting my statement.

"No whingeing," I think as I followed him up to the house. "That's pretty good at five."

I recall that Julie, at that age, would also have recognised reason. Like daughter, like son. Identical strong hair and dark brown eyes. I drop a kiss on the crown of his head as he climbs the steps to the front door, and he pulls away, a little surprised by my display of affection. But he gives a chuckle, as if he is apologising for how a man has to act.

After lunch, I say, "Mum's left us a shopping list. Shall we go to the supermarket?"

"No," he replies

I make a face at him. "We'll go anyway."

He pushes back his chair. "Don't want to."

I hear him drag his tricycle from under the stairs and into the garden. My heart goes out to such defiance and I wonder if his rebellious spirit will resolve into courage or despair, when he is a man. I wander across the sitting room, reaching to pick up a framed snapshot of Julie's husband. He is on the beach and there is a towel slung carelessly around his neck. He has a kind face. Robert, too, had that kindness. Until he discovered my infidelity . . .

"I know I'm fifteen years older than you, Caroline. But why Mike Davison? He's just a boy . . ."

I had wanted to tell him of my emotional desert and of my resentment at being needed only at needful times. I had wanted to tell him how a young man's love and laughter had aroused me to a point of no return.

"I can't give you an answer," I had said. "It just happened."

Carefully, I replaced Jonathan's photo, glad at least that I can be useful in this happy marriage of my daughter, by caring for Matthew twice a week, so that she can hold a part-time job. And, now, these regular meetings with Sarah. I smile as I remember the two schoolgirls. Always the best of friends. They had always been together. Now in these past eight weeks they are together again. Matthew has entered the room and I am deliberately casual.

"If you'd like to come to the supermarket, mister, we'll have tea afterwards in The Copper Kettle."

His nod conveys acquiescence, rather than capitulation and I long to hold him in my arms and tell him how much I love him. Instead I chuck him under the chin.

In the crowded cafe the beehive murmur of voices lulls me into dreaminess, as I sense there is no need to converse with a small boy who is demolishing an eclair. A middle-aged woman stops at our table.

"Aren't you Mrs Crawford? I was Julie's drama teacher at school. "Perhaps you don't remember me?"

I assure her that I do.

"Julie's been married for six years."

I indicate Matthew, who glances briefly in our direction, before chasing a blob of cream around his plate. "You helped her understand the Arts," I continue, "and I've always been grateful to you."

The teacher looks pleased.

"It was a good year. A few of the girls had real promise: Joanna Reid, Laura McDonald, Sarah Lynch."

"Sarah is Julie's great friend . . ." I begin.

Spontaneously she interrupts me.

"Of course, I remember! Sarah was so fond of Julie. She's in Africa, now, as you know."

I stare at her. "Africa? She can't be."

"She's been there for nearly a year Mrs Crawford, and will be for some time. Our headmistress heard from her only a few days ago, apologising for not attending our reunion."

I clutch at straws. "A letter?"

Sarah could have come home since writing it, I think frantically.

The teacher glances at her watch.

"It was a phone call, actually. She is producing a film in Kenya."

She is brisk and decisive. There is no reason to doubt her. I leave the cafe with my grandson's small hand in mine, unable to concentrate on his animated chatter. He is just like Julie, whose energy was always renewed by eating. Like mother, like son—like mother, like daughter . . .

I open the door of Julie's house and go through to the sitting room. With my heightened emotions, I notice for the first time how the furnishings—the combination of shapes and colours—are a sure reflection of my own. I recall the way Julie walks and talks; her addiction to books and drama; her inherited obstinacy. And—dismayingly—her weaknesses. Matthew is tugging at my hand.

"I'm thirsty."

I pour orange juice, trying to think but I can only see the morning's expectation in Julie's eyes, and Jonathan's face merging into Robert's. When I hear the key in the front door, I am peeling potatoes, my mind clicking and whirring to explosive levels. I walk slowly into the hall, wiping my hands on the kitchen towel, drying fastidiously between my fingers and up my wrists, like a woman weeping. Julie is sitting on the stairs listening to Matthew. She looks up as I appear, her lips parted in a relaxed and lovely smile. I see the glow of excitement in her flushed face and the unusual brightness of her eyes, and I am conscious of an almost physical pain. Then, controlling my voice, I say:

"Did you have a good day?"

Waiting for Sebastian

First published 1990
Woman Summer Special

His blue eyes probe my mind. I decide not to mention this morning's phone call.

"So you won't be coming with me next month?" he says.

"No, I won't," I tell him, "since you ask. Anyway, I can't get the time off work at the moment. But I might, if you ever get sent to the Mediterranean."

Why does he only ask me when he's going to the north of England? Why can't he get me invited to Rome or Vienna or St. Tropez? Or does he have someone there who I mustn't meet? He laughs, just like Christopher Reeves laughs, with thrown-back head. He has the same even teeth; the same struggling-to-keep-boyish look, with straight dark hair. Don't think I wouldn't settle for the Christopher Reeve image, especially if it grows old along with me; the best is yet to come sort of thing! Unfortunately, men who look like that usually want to stay like that. The trouble starts from there. They pull in their stomach muscles to hide the tell-tale roll. They wear hip-hugging trousers and slim-cut shirts. Granted, for a long time they maintain their hold and I can vouch for that with Sebastian when I observe the women straighten a little and see the instant softness around their mouths and the anticipation in their eyes, if he joins a group of people at the party. Again, I repeat:

"No, I don't want to go. Ask me when you get sent to Italy or somewhere."

I still don't mention the phone call. For a moment I think I see a shadow of disappointment in his face, but his expression is unemotional as he says:

122

"Sorry you can't come. But don't worry about it. I'll have plenty to do."

Is that relief I hear in his voice? Straight away, I am suspicious. Men would say to me: 'Now, why are you reacting like that? Sebastian's being more than reasonable. He asked you to go with him, didn't he?' Women would say: 'He's not very upset about you turning him down, is he? There's something going on.'

Of course, with Sebastian, things have been going on for a long while before I met him. He had quite a reputation. I've not been with him for five years without knowing that within this man is the perennial peacock boy. The trouble is, I love him. But I've only just discovered it.

This evening he is utterly kind and charming. I've been extra busy at the office where I'm an assistant manager, and he insists on cooking the meal. Because Sebastian is arranging the occasion, the jasmine has opened its buds to glow seductively in the lamplight through the uncurtained window bay where he's laid the table with the checked cloth. The richness of his special Bolognese sauce steals headily from the kitchen and he enters the sitting room carrying a bottle of claret, a striped butcher's apron around his waist. With a flourish he escorts me to the table, smiling down at me with those white, white teeth, while the dark hair falls endearingly on his forehead. Oh, I'll settle for this, Sebastian. I'll settle for the pink rose in the silver vase and the touch of your lovely fingers as you bend to kiss the nape of my neck. I'll settle for the way you look at me and give me your undivided attention. Because now is now and tomorrow's reality is a lifetime away.

"Have I overcooked the spaghetti?" He is anxious that my silence could mean he has fallen below his usual high standard.

"It's perfect." I assure him. "Best ever."

I don't mention this morning's phone call.

I've had other friends from time to time. There is an agreement between us that allows freedom. If one of us falls in love, Sebastian said from the start, the other will accept it. Sebastian said! But Sebastian is not in love.

When I moved in with him, I'd been glad of our arrangement. We'd demanded nothing of each other. No commitments. No stipulations. I had a broken engagement behind me and, for the time being, Sebastian had offered me a bolt-hole. I'd even brought him down to meet my parents, where he'd been totally relaxed. I'd watched my mother's usual reserve melt like an ice floe in the sun, while my father had forgotten to pass comment on our relationship, which is quite unlike him.

"Seb's always been a bit wild," my brother told me, "but he's a good sort. He'll settle down one day. He thinks you're great."

"Oh, I know," I grinned, aching inside.

"You're what he needs" he went on. "You're a rock."

"With a smashed engagement behind me?" I said.

"You were the one with the sense to break it off," he said. "Ian was the wrong one for you, he was too predictable. Rocks don't need rocks."

Sebastian sometimes says: 'Never leave me.' But more often he says: 'If you meet anyone else Carol, I wouldn't stand in your way.'

I haven't heard him make the last statement for quite a while and lately, he seems to seek my company more and more. But leopards don't change their spots, do they? *Do they?* The phone call had been this morning. The voice was high and sweet. After listening, I'd said:

"Yes, of course you can come round to see me, if that's what you want. But how did you know I share this flat with Sebastian?"

"I work in his office," she'd said. "I know he's got a meeting this evening, hasn't he? Could I come then?"

When I answered the knock, I was overwhelmed, not so much by her prettiness, as by her extreme youth. She was thin and daffodil-straight, with smooth luxurious auburn hair. I noticed how her fine-boned hands were tightly clenched. Indoors, she sat on the edge of a chair, with a beaker of coffee going cold beside her.

"How long have you been with the firm?" I asked.
"Six months. I went straight from school to the clerical department."

She reached to take a sip of coffee.

"I love him," she said, and my heart went out to the brave tilt of her small chin and the dark rings beneath her eyes.

My voice was gentle. "Has he encouraged you at all?"

She twisted the strap of her shoulder bag. She was painfully honest, her face flushed pink.

"No. He hardly seems to notice me but I know I can change that. I wait for him outside the office."

How did Sebastian react to that, I wondered. She answered my unspoken question.

"He began to worry because sometimes it was quite late and the streets were dark, but I didn't mind that. I think he thought I might get attacked."

"And then?" I prompted.

"He started to see me to my home, because I told him I'd be outside the office every evening until he left the building. I think he felt responsible for me. I wanted him to feel like that."

I closed my eyes at the sheer determination of this vulnerable girl. When I opened them, she was staring at me.

"Why are you holding him?" she asked me. "I know I can make him love me. Anyway, surely you're too old for him?"

"I'm three years younger than he is!"

Despite my sympathy, I was irritated by the arrogance of youth.

"And he's about twelve years older than you. Have you thought of that?"

"That's different," she said. "I prefer older men."

Softly, I asked her: "Did he tell you that I was holding him?"

"He said he couldn't think of leaving you, because you would never let him go."

I stood up. I felt absurdly happy.

"Would you believe he's never asked me to?" I said. "You see, I'm his rock . . . his anchor."

After she'd gone, I had a shower and put on a new silk dress I'd been saving for goodness knows how long. When Sebastian was due home from his meeting, I drew back the curtains and stared out at the mauve shadows of the evening. Windows were blooming with light around the little square and I felt suddenly warm and confident as I thought about Sebastian and all the ways he'd lately shown he loved me. Perhaps my suspicions of these last few years with him had been unfounded. Perhaps they hadn't. But I had no right to continue to doubt him. I thought of Sebastian's rejection of the daffodil girl. I knew, now, that I had come into his life at the right time. After a while, I saw him walking briskly along the lamplit street. When he reached our steps, he looked up as if I had called his name, and I opened the window and leaned out, ignoring the chill in the air.

"I love you," I said.

The expression on his face made me fly across the room and down the stairs. He was standing in the hall, waiting, and I ran straight into his wide, welcoming arms.

Pattern For Life

First published 2nd July 1990
Woman

David asks:

"Don't you think we ought to go on holiday with other people now and again, Rachel?"

"But why?" I say. "We've always gone with George and Poppy."

The four of us left college in the same year. Almost immediately, flame-haired Poppy had married serious, dogmatic George. I think it was because she had a definite preference for brainy men. Soon afterwards, I said to David:

"This could mean you and I are meant for each other, couldn't it? And then we'd be a foursome again."

He frowned. "Aren't you being insular? There's a world out there that won't include George and Poppy all the time."

I smiled at him, mentally fixing our wedding date. I didn't need anyone else to intrude on our group and I was surprised David had even mentioned it. But then he'd been moody ever since Poppy's marriage, so I assumed he missed our friends as much as I did and would be glad to start his career in the market town where they now lived.

Soon after the birth of Poppy's daughter, I had a son, enabling me to dream of circles within circles on my private pond. James and Louisa. Caviar and champagne. Wine and roses. The first time I hinted at such a possibility, David became unreasonably angry.

"For heaven's sake, Rachel. If you're determined to programme their lives, at least try to set wider boundaries. You're a pattern-maker, did you know that?"

"There's nothing wrong with that, David," I replied.

For me, the four of us and the two kids are all I need. If dissension creeps in, I usually refuse to acknowledge it. Until a while ago. It started in a small way, with Poppy not responding to George's rather ponderous jokes so that David and I felt embarrassed for him and tried to laugh. Poppy just stared, stony-faced. In the following weeks, the atmosphere between them built up to a new level where I wanted to step in. But David was adamant.

"If they've got a problem, they must work out their own solution. Just leave it, Rachel."

One evening, when Poppy and I are in the final stages of preparing a curry for our regular supper party, she announces:

"You do realise that George is going to be late tonight?"

I'm casual. "Held up at the laboratory, is he?"

"Probably not, but he'll still be late," repeats Poppy. I glance at her. She leans against the worktop for a moment, flexing her shoulders and yawning, bringing alive the sleek animal on her plastic bib-apron.

"I'd really like to know what's wrong between you two," I say, hoping I don't sound too eager.

"Are you sitting comfortably?" She moves away from the worktop and pauses for several seconds. "I'm pretty certain there's someone else."

"George unfaithful?" I exclaim. "I don't believe it!"

"Neither did I, at first."

She straightens and watches me, her eyes lazy and faintly mocking.

"George is so serious and academic," I protest.

Poppy moves to sniff the contents of the saucepan. "Which would go down well with a serious and academic girl, don't you think? I've known for ages," she says. "George is a dark horse. He can't resist a beautiful girl, especially if she also happens to be an intellectual."

I'm indignant for her.

"He's not being very fair, is he? You came out of college with flying colours."

"Okay, so I'm intelligent. But I'm not in his class. George's a superbrain! I realised soon after I married him that we never really meet on the same level. It's as much my fault as his."

There's a ring at the front door and we hear David talking to George in the hall. I pick up a dish of salad.

"What'll you do, Poppy?"

Her smile is derisive. "Well, I think I'll just play the waiting game. So the group will be safe for a while."

I try to hide my relief, but it doesn't fool her.

"I knew that would please you," she says.

She pushes open the swing doors and my answer dies on my lips as I follow her through into the dining room.

Halfway into supper, I refer to the lovely Devon cottage that we'd booked for two weeks the previous September.

"Fine with me, if you want to book it again." David doesn't look up from his plate as he speaks.

"All right with you, George?" drawls Poppy.

He shrugs and nods.

"The children loved the moors and beaches last time." I'm aware that I'm sounding over-enthusiastic. "And we all got on so well, didn't we?"

George glances at me. He's slightly pompous but allows himself a grin.

"We should be grateful we've all stayed friends for so long. Statistically, we've defied the odds."

There's boredom in Poppy's heavy-lidded eyes. She looks at George, but she's speaking to me.

"United we stand! Rachel won't even allow us to divide, let alone fall. Will you Rachel?"

George frowns at her. "No need to be sarcastic, Poppy. Rachel's worked extremely hard to keep us all together."

I'm slightly uneasy at his emphasis on my role, but I say:

"Yes, we'll always stay friends."

"But of course," murmurs Poppy. "Long live the group!"

David's fork falls on his plate heavily enough to startle us. I glimpse anger in his eyes, but he's smiling as he turns to Poppy.

"Right little cynic, aren't you?"

She laughs at him, raising her glass of wine and, not for the first time, I feel that they've moved away from us.

"Did you know things were going wrong between them?" I ask David that night. "I didn't really believe Poppy when she told me."

"The only reason for that," he replies, plumping up his pillows, "is because you didn't want to. It threatened your way of life. Who are you concerned for, Rachel? George and Poppy? Or yourself?"

"All of us," I answer.

"Ah, yes." He speaks slowly. "The group!"

"The trouble is," I say, "George is much too brainy for Poppy. Don't you agree?"

He speaks quietly. "No."

"Don't be silly, David. He's a brilliant scientist."

His eyes are cold.

"George is so wrapped up in his projects, he hardly notices when Poppy's around. Don't you think someone as warm as she is resents that?"

"It works both ways." I say, sulkily. "I don't think she really understands him."

He sighs. "I'd rather have Poppy's intelligence and shrewdness any day, than one half of George's brilliance. I hope she goes back to her career as soon as she possibly can."

"You've never said that about me, David. How do you know I don't want to go back to work?"

He doesn't reply.

"Well, you and I won't ever contemplate parting, will we David?"

I wonder if I've misheard his low voice.

"We should never be sure of anything, Rachel."

The sun shines every day. The moors smell of wild thyme. We sit around in the evenings playing cards or talking. The talks often end in merriment and fooling, as they did when we were all at college. Sometimes I'd hold a particular scene in my mind, wanting our love and laughter to be safe and impregnable. I wanted it always to be like this. On our last morning, while the children go riding, the four of us decide to swim in a tarn.

"We won't bother with swimsuits," says Poppy.

"Oh, come now," says George.

I stare at her. "You're not serious are you?"

"Oh, I am! I am!"

David laughs and throws his arm across Poppy's shoulders with an easy familiarity that makes me glance quickly away from them. As we approach the pool we see a couple below us, their nude bodies pink, their breath coming in gasps as they clamber up the bank. The man draws the girl towards him, holding her close. A probe of sunlight through the backdrop of silver birches makes me think, fleetingly, of a stage.

"Well. that's that," says Poppy, folding her arms and staring. "Mustn't disturb young love!"

My cheeks scarlet, I see her tilted head and her lips parted by her tongue, as if she were assessing a painting in a gallery. She doesn't move.

"I'm not staying," I tell her. "We'll embarrass them."

"I agree," says George.

Poppy sits down on the heather and wraps her arms around her drawn-up knees. Her hair blows about her like a red cloud.

"I want my swim," she says.

"So do I," says David, stretching out beside her. "But you two needn't wait. We'll meet you in the pub at midday?"

I stumble up the rough pathway and I notice George is silently keeping pace with me. I don't dare to look back at Poppy and David.

Towards the end of September, Louisa joins my son at school, and Poppy secures a post in the out-patient unit of the local hospital, despite my warning that it might not be wise to resume her career while her child's so young. She just laughs, in that elusive, mocking way of hers.

David accuses me of interfering.

"For goodness sake, Rachel. Why is it that you always try to manipulate people?" he says.

"David, I don't understand you. I only try to cement our relationship as a group."

"We're not bricks, Rachel. We're people!"

His eyes slide away from me and I see his unsmiling mouth. The feeling lodges in me, like a shred of metal, that he's thinking of another person in another place and another sort of love. The holidays are over and tonight it's my turn again for our weekly meal. As it's David's birthday, I've allowed the children to stay up.

Noticing they are already beginning to quarrel, I warn them:

"Five minutes more."

David and Poppy are studying a brochure on interior design. George stands near the children, twirling his glass. He glances over at me, his sombre expression replaced for a moment by an unexpected boyish grin. I smile fondly at him.

"We've had a great holiday, haven't we?" he says, compelling me to look at him.

"Wonderful," I say.

"No, not wonderful. Far from it. But good, certainly. We should be glad of that, at the very least."

I feel nervous. "I don't know what you're trying to say."

I turn to the children, but his voice is like a hand on my arm. The dark eyes are watchful.

"Yes, you do. Surely you realise how everyone's changed? How dangerous it can be to cling to an ideal?" he says.

"That's my security," I protest. "I rely on a life pattern."

"But you can't have patterns for *people,* Rachel."

I push aside my surge of fear and my sudden longing for someone to hold me.

"You sound like David," I tell him.

"Oh, Rachel, I just don't want you to be hurt."

Fingers tug at mine as a child's voice interrupts us. I stare down at the sweet face of Louisa and the rather sullen features of James, then my gaze wanders to David, who's talking to Poppy with a concentration that makes me conscious of their closeness. I'm instantly aware that the brochure they were reading is on the floor. A stone skeeters across the surface of my mind, but I walk firmly with the children towards the door. George offers to stay upstairs until they're in bed. I give him an affectionate kiss and stand for a moment on the bottom step, disappointed he didn't turn when he reached the top. Later, I stand in my dining room, admiring the gleaming crystal on the table and in the centre the candle, standing sleek as a rocket, on its flower base.

"This is my life, my home," I murmur quietly to myself. "Nothing's going to spoil our lives together. Why did I ever imagine it for even one treacherous minute?"

I lean to light the candle. The four chairs are waiting.

'My beautiful home,' I think, 'my lovely possessions.'

Smiling, I turn to call everyone into dinner.

The Web

His irritation at her phone call was already turning to excitement when he drove through the night to her lakeside house. It was the second time she had ever pleaded with him. The first time was when she had begged him not to leave her. He swung off the road up a tree-lined path and immediately saw her in the open doorway. He parked the car and walked towards her. He felt a gossamer touch from her fingers, as she said,

"I heard your car, darling. Were you alone when I phoned?"

"I was. Apart from a few dancing girls!"

He thrust his hands into his pockets, scowling at her. "I thought I made it clear you were not to get in touch with me?"

"I know, but I needed your help. Anyway, you came, didn't you?"

He was aware of her triumphant smile as he walked past her to the sitting-room.

"I was curious, Janet, that's all."

Still smiling, she followed him.

"How accustomed you are to this house, Peter. You belong to it."

She crossed to a side-table and his aggression faded in his familiar arousal at her movements. She returned to him with filled glasses.

"Where's your husband," he asked. "At one of his meetings?"

"He didn't go to work today. He was drunk, as usual."

"You mean he's here? Now?"

"Yes, darling."

He choked on his brandy.

"What are you thinking of! Is he asleep?"

She was motionless against the backdrop of the fire.

"No, Peter." Her eyes were watchful. "He isn't asleep. He's dead!"

When he didn't reply, she formed her words as though explaining to a child.

"I poisoned him. I had to, you see."

He slammed down his glass and moved towards the hall.

"Goodbye, Janet. I'm in no mood for one of your black jokes."

Something metallic was pressed into his hand.

"The key to the study, darling. If you don't believe me, see for yourself."

In the shadowed library, his stomach contracted, as he bent over the stiffened body. Locking the door behind him, he retraced his steps, to thrust the key into her outstretched hand.

"For God's sake, woman. Were you out of your mind?"

With her back to the flames, she looked taller than he remembered. Her gaze was almost impersonal, her voice casual.

"We had one of our arguments this morning, and he started shouting and screaming, so I went out for the rest of the day. When I got back, he was waiting for me, and it was obvious he's done some hard drinking. I tried to run upstairs, but he became violent and began to hit me."

She lifted the hair from the side of her face.

"Look."

He felt compassion. "You should have left him years ago, before he was this bad."

With a dry laugh, she said, "He'd have followed me wherever I went. With his money, he could have me traced."

Sick at the thought of the body in the other room, he forced himself to ask,

"How did you poison him?"

"I told him to go to the bathroom. I'd had the stuff hidden in there for weeks. When he quietened down for a while, I poured it into his whisky."

"Didn't he notice the taste?"

"He was too far gone. He just gulped it down."

"I must inform the police, Janet. You do realise that?"

She was at the telephone before him.

"I don't think I could survive if they sent me to prison. I'd kill myself first."

He believed her. She was not a woman who could accept humiliation. He was again motivated by pity, recalling the intensity of their relationship. He heard himself saying,

"What do you want me to do?"

"I have a scheme," she said.

He turned away from the telephone.

"Oh, I'm sure you have, Janet. I'm sure you have . . ."

He was glad she insisted on blanket-wrapping the body without his help.

"I've tied it securely," she said. "You'll find some heavy weights in the boat-house."

The lake was tapestried in black and silver, as he watched his burden splinter the surface and vanish beneath it. He returned the boat to its moorings and drove back to the house. The clouds peeled away from the moon, as she met him.

"How do you feel, now that it's over?" she asked.

"All I've done is to dispose of a dead body," he said, "but you have to live with being a murderer."

He paused. The expression on her face puzzled him. "I'll not be seeing you after this. I mean it."

"Oh. I think you'll be staying, darling!"

He stared at her in disgust, then turned away.

"It was only a knock-out drug, Peter. It paralyses for a few hours! . . ."

She walked towards him, holding out her arms . . .

Untitled

Which of us can say that peace is in our heads and in our understanding?
Who can say with certainty that the fingers stilled and the breath slowed and deepened
Is a state of peace
Or a prelude to war.
On the journey down the Dark Well, nerves screaming, to emergence, later, under washed skies.
To hear the thunder of the waves along the shore.
To be free.
The release of the spirit quietens the body's reflexes.
Colours are brighter and then again, are muted within the spectrum of discernibility.
We'll share a pie and quaff some ale and nod our heads to show how wise we are.
For words oft said have no more meaning than the flare of a lonely star.
. . . Go paint a room,
Write a book,
WAR AND PEACE—has that been done before?
I know . . . we'll call it
PEACE AND WAR!

Long Ago in Ireland

Mrs Duffy's had her fifth.
The midwife leaves,
settling her woollen shawl around her head.
Tom Duffy climbs the stairs to see his son.

The town is stark. No garden flowers; no trees;
no soft-hung curtains
Showing rosy light.
The oil lamp flickers into life only when families meet when
work is done.
To eat potato snowballs boiled in skins.

Outside the town, grey ruin walls, with quivering ivy hiding
all the scars,
Was once an abbey.
High on a hill a celtic cross
Marks Patrick's saintly progress through this land
Of warm soft rain and grass,
so lush and green it calms the soul.

In bogland tracts, the beckoning cotton flowers
Entice the traveller to dark unfathomed depths,
Atlantic mists to be their shrouding sheet.

At morning mass, in long sleeved frocks and suits of
bombazine
The congregation kneel in awe before their vigilant priest.
Like children they obey. His word is God's.

In two long rows sit laundered nuns, with quiet hands on
somber skirts,

As water lilies lie on black glass ponds. Thin candletips soar
upwards
To the wooden-faced Madonna, holding her tiny Christ.

Beneath the churchyard yews, the blank eyed angels applaud
with lifted arms
The family sacrifice which set them there,
atop the glass-domed flowers
And hummocked earth.

Mrs Clooney is by her window.
Her eyes are fixed on distant hills,
their gentle summits veiled with gorse.
Still young, this girl, yet prematurely old with pallid face and
wispy locks
Escaping hairpinned bun.

Her brood of chicken children share her fingers
Their downy heads nudging her skirted legs.
A smile touches her eyes,
eluding her mouth. A baby cries; a man swears;
A pot boils over. The woman turns
Her thoughts of home lost in a splinter of time.

Around the working farms,
the thrusting corn awaits the reaper.
The rabbits in their straw-stalk forest, scrabble for grain with
dainty claws.
Above their heads,
the fragile poppies are held in captive swirls.
Small creatures prowl and others sleep with rustling sounds
and murmurs.
A climbing moon is lanced by an oak tree leaf.

The seasons pass. The corn is cut. The porridge cauldron filled.
The fuschias bow once more to summer's prelude, each
skirted bud in pirouette.

Another year of life. And–praise the Lord!
The fruitful Mrs Duffy's had her sixth!

Saturday Daughters

Morning Story
19th March 1985

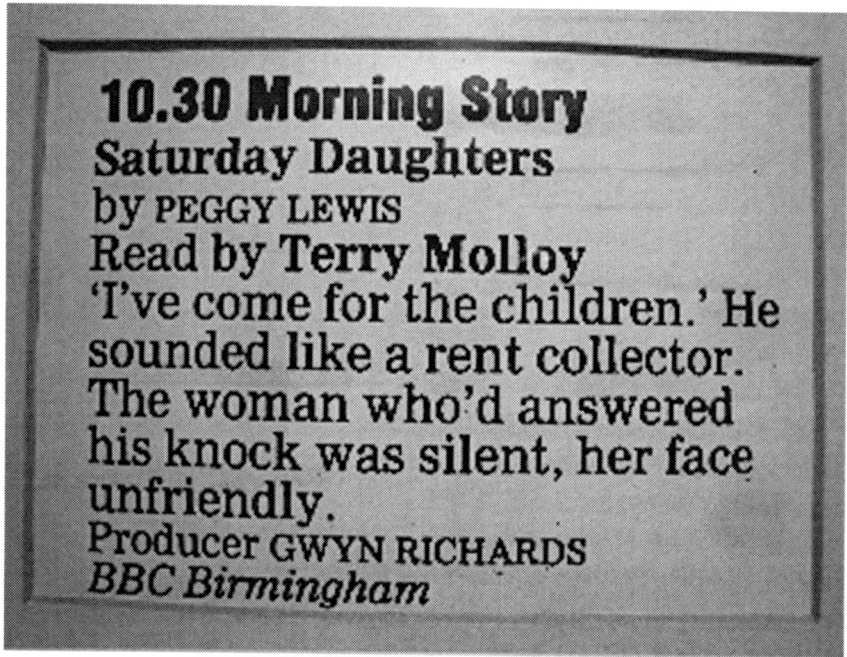

> **10.30 Morning Story**
> **Saturday Daughters**
> by PEGGY LEWIS
> Read by **Terry Molloy**
> 'I've come for the children.' He
> sounded like a rent collector.
> The woman who'd answered
> his knock was silent, her face
> unfriendly.
> Producer GWYN RICHARDS
> *BBC Birmingham*

"I've come for the children."

He sounded like a rent collector. The woman who had answered his knock was silent, her face unfriendly.

"Saturday's my day for them," he continued, resentful that she was forcing an unnecessary explanation from him.

"Madeleine," she called without turning her head, "he's here."

"Well for goodness sake, mother, let him in."

He walked through the hall into the familiar room and stood with faint awkwardness on the patterned carpet. The younger

143

woman wore a dress of emerald green with enamelled, scarlet circles covering the lobes of her ears.

"They're getting ready. I'd asked mother to take them out, until Josephine reminded me you were coming."

Her words were casual, with no hint of apology. She peered at herself in the mirror above the cluttered mantelshelf and patted her lacquered hair. A smile softened the lines of her mouth, eluding her eyes. It was not for him. Her mother, who had followed him from the hallway, was standing with folded arms, regarding him with cold hostility. He attempted to speak politely to her, but his tone was indifferent.

"Sorry you had a wasted journey. I can only manage Saturdays."

She sniffed, but didn't reply. Instead, she picked up her hat and skewered it to her crimped hair with a vicious pin.

"I'll be off to the shops then Maddy, as I'm not needed. I'll see the little ones later."

She ignored him as she left the room with her daughter, but he was unperturbed. He had always found it easy to forget her.

When Madeleine returned, he surreptitiously studied this stranger, wondering if they were ever in love. She was predictably defensive for her mother.

"She can't forgive you for the divorce, Jake. It's hard to accept things at her age. I wish you'd try to be warmer to her."

He prowled to the window, oblivious to her words, anxious for the children to appear. He looked at his watch, seeing the day slip by. Her lips tightened at the gesture.

"You never liked waiting for anyone, did you? Why don't you just sit for a moment and be patient!"

When they came downstairs, the girls walked to him with quiet voices, conscious of Madeleine standing by.

"Where are we going, Daddy?"

He reached for them and buried his face in their hair, smelling their healthy scalps, revelling in the smoothness of their skins, realising how hungry he had been for the feel of their thin arms. Madeleine was watching them and, because

144

he glimpsed boredom in her gaze, he pushed his daughters away, pretending he was gasping for air.

"You want to know where we're going, do you?"

Josephine beckoned to him and he bent to her. Her pansy-dark eyes moved close to his, as though she was peeping through a window into his mind.

"In my crystal ball, I see the circus!"

He stood, his tallness dominating the low-ceilinged room.

"Not today, pet. We're going to lunch and the cinema. Then, maybe, a boat on the lake, if we can fit it all in. How about that?"

The children were excited, running ahead of him down the front path fighting to be the first to get into the car. He glanced at Madeleine. Without interest, he asked,

"How's Neil?"

Her reply was equally flat. "He's fine. He's asked me to marry him."

"And will you?"

She half shrugged. "Probably. I'm thinking about it."

She waved to the children and, when he turned at the gate, she had already closed the door. He was vaguely annoyed that she hadn't stayed there to watch them leave.

Josephine leaned her chin on the back of his seat, as he started the car.

"Will Rachel be having supper with us this evening?"

"Sure to be, pet. She gets back from College about five."

Daisy joined in. "I wish she was my teacher. Will she always be at your flat?"

He thought of Rachel's youth and independence. He thought of his own uncertainty about their future together. He smiled at Daisy in the driving mirror.

"Of course she will, darling. Of course."

After the film, they decided it was time for an hour on the boating lake. The placid waters were fringed by woodland and, beneath the canopy of branches, the children chased a darting squirrel. A single probe of sunlight held them as they stopped to look back at him, bluebells falling from their fingers, and he longed to tell them he would be with them through all their growing years. But his daughters, in their short, bright skirts, had skipped beyond the trees and were waiting for him at the boathouse. The surface of the lake was skeined with pink as the man leaned from the window of his hut, insisting they could only have thirty minutes before he packed up.

"We don't mind," Josephine assured him. "We're both hungry, so an hour would have been too long anyway."

He stooped to kiss the top of her dark head. Josie was the kind one; the thoughtful one. The foil to quicksilver Daisy.

The girls sat, with wooden-doll legs, at one end of the boat, their hands clutching the sides as he manoevured from the edge. They circled the island, where the water geese woke from their huddled sleep, raising their long, starched necks and opening their beaks in soundless indignation. A mottled quill floated on the metallic surface and Daisy stretched her arm towards it, rocking the boat. Josephine jumped to her feet when the oars slipped from Jake's fingers. As Daisy tipped over the side, the disapproving geese fussed their wings and took to the lake in matronly convoy.

Jake had known Rachel would be brisk and efficient when they arrived at his flat. Her eyes grew wide as she saw them standing in the hall, but she asked no questions. A hot bath for Daisy was followed by a high tea, while the children recounted their rescue by the boat-hire man in his motorised dinghy. Rachel listened without interrupting, laughing when she heard how Jake had hauled Daisy into the boat by the waistband of her skirt. He felt extravagantly grateful to this girl with the smooth, brown hair, sitting across the table from him, her chin cupped in her hand, smiling at his daughters.

"They love you," he whispered to her later, in the kitchen. "It was good of you to cook their favourite food."

She studied him for a moment, her hands motionless in the washing-up water, but she said nothing as she turned away.

When he drove them home, Daisy stayed in her borrowed, towelling mini-robe, while Josephine carried the damp things in a plastic bag.

Madeleine over-reacted and accused him of being negligent, as her mother waited nearby in unconcealed antagonism.

"She might have drowned. You know she can't swim yet."

The children were huge-eyed as they heard the angry words. Aware of their worried faces, he struggled to stay calm.

In a far-away voice, Josephine said, "It wasn't Daddy's fault. We stood up and rocked the boat."

He wanted to hug her for her loyalty. He longed to tell them both that the day had not been spoiled; that, because they were together, it had been a warm and perfect time. Instead, he closed his eyes in frustration and bent to kiss them on their flushed cheeks. They whispered,

"It's been very nice, thank you," in subdued voices, and Daisy cried a little.

"You've kept them out too late," said Madeleine. "They're overtired."

He didn't heed the implication that he was entirely to blame, as he stood in the hall watching them climb the stairs, his gaze searching the shadows even when they were out of sight.

He was still there, motionless, when Madeleine handed him the towelling wrap. He took it from her and left in silence.

For two days, even when he was occupied at work, he was depressed but, as the week went by, he looked forward, refusing to allow his fears to affect him.

Occasionally, Rachel was restless when he talked too much about the children. He tried to tell her how he felt.

"I'm so proud of them. They're wonderful kids."

She shook her head.

"You expect too much from them, love. You have to let go. Children are scared by possessiveness. It makes them anxious."

He smiled at her.

"When you have children of your own, you'll understand."

"Don't patronise me, Jake."

Puzzled, as she moved away from him, he said, "I will always love you."

She turned in the doorway, her face expressionless.

"You think I don't know that?"

There was something in her voice which he vaguely resented.

"Aren't you being rather cynical?" he asked.

"A cynic is what an idealist calls a realist, Jake."

Gently, the door closed behind her. Later, in the fading light of evening, she placed a casserole in the microwave and said,

"I want to talk to you, but I don't think you are going to like what I have to say."

He was opening the wine, so her gravity did not immediately impress him.

"How do you know I won't?" He was deliberately flippant.

"I just know."

She was so definite that he stopped what he was doing and looked across at her. She was half sitting on the kitchen table, toying with a lettuce leaf, wrapping it around her finger.

"I don't want marriage or babies, Jake. At least, not yet."

He stifled the fear which had been with him since he had met her. Then he smiled, a man-smile, before turning from the steadiness in her grey eyes.

"Rachel, my dear, you're young. You'll change your mind. Most women want children early in their lives."

"Well, I don't! My mother had six children and I was the eldest."

He knew she was staring, wanting him to face her. With painstaking deliberation, he wiped away an invisible trickle from the bottle of wine. He straightened, still avoiding her gaze.

"Don't worry. Lots of girls react like this, Rachel."

Humouring her, he repeated, "You're young. You'll soon have different ideas. You'll see."

She slid from the table and walked over to him.

"If I do it could be years from now. And it may not be with you."

Her voice was calm, but there was a kindness there, also. "I'm not ready yet to settle down. Don't you understand that?"

She stopped speaking, as he hunched away from her, refusing to listen to her. She watched him as he hummed a tune, laying the cloth and setting out the glasses with quick, agitated movements. After a moment, she quietly left the room.

The day before he was due to collect the children, Madeleine phoned. Alarmed by the unaccustomed call he asked, "Is Daisy OK?"

"She had a dreadful cold, of course, which isn't surprising after what happened . . ."

Begrudgingly she added, "Anyway, she's better now."

"What time shall I come for them tomorrow?"

He tried to control the impatience which was always there when he spoke to her.

"I thought perhaps I'd take them to the zoo."

"That's why I've rung."

Her tone implied she could have no other reason for communication.

"Neil has the weekend free and we're planning to go out. The four of us."

"But surely he works on a Saturday, Madeleine?"

He heard the exasperated sigh.

"Well not this week. So, if you don't mind having an extra visit some other time . . ."

His anger jumbled his protest.

"I do mind, if you want to know. Neil can take you out alone. Saturday's my day for the children."

Madeleine called to someone and, almost immediately, a soft, breathless voice came on the line.

"Hallo, Daddy?"

"Ah! Josie. I'm looking forward to seeing you tomorrow, pet."

He was sure he could hear Madeleine whispering in the background. When Josephine spoke again, she sounded nervous.

"Uncle Neil has got a Saturday free, for once, and he wants to take us all to the Palladium. He's bought tickets."

He felt betrayed.

"Are you there, Daddy?"

"Yes. Yes, I'm here." Disappointment dulled his reply.

"Of course, I can't stop you, Josie. Do you really want to go?"

Her response was instant and joyful. He tried to speak but the words wouldn't form. Madeleine took over, demanding and impatient.

Slowly, with infinite care, he replaced the receiver.

Never Go Back

Morning short story
Thursday 30ᵗʰ April 1959

It was quite an ordinary signpost. But it barred my way across
the wide road as decisively as a barricade thrown hastily in
front of my car. I had been driving almost automatically from
Exeter making for the Midlands. My mind had been forming
and shaping the report I would submit to my firm on the
business deal I had just pulled off. So it must have been some
deep-frozen impulse which prompted me to take a rather
more roundabout, but undoubtedly prettier route, through
the rolling countryside of Somerset.

The bent little signpost was faintly appealing, and it
pushed its small lettered snout out of the hedge with an air
of apology for being compelled to point out the existence of
a village leading off the main road. Abruptly I drew to a stop
near the high banking, my mind groping for some explanation.
What sudden twist in my thinking had urged me to take a
road I hadn't travelled for fifteen years? But even as my hand
reached for the starter, and I turned slowly down towards the
village, I knew the answer.

I had meant to come!

High, untidy hedges flanked and narrowed the lane but
here and there, through a tumbledown gateway, I saw the
pink drifts of willowherb swirling in and out of the woods
and coppices. As I breasted the hill overlooking the village,
the morning sun collected the last pools of mist lingering in
the valleys. It seemed as though a curtain was swept aside,
and I could take in at one glance the rich pastureland of the
place I had lived in so many years ago.

Nothing had changed. Nothing at all. Except perhaps
for the television aerials on the cottage rooftops. The church

clock showed a quarter past twelve, as I parked the car in the dusty little square, and–ducking my head–I peered into the doorway of the Bird in Hand. It was cool and dim and, at first, my eyes–blinded by sunlight–refused to focus on anything but an orange bonfire of marigolds lighting a dark corner. Then I heard a cheerful voice in the passage outside, and a large red-faced man shouldered into the bar with a trayload of glasses. He banged them on the counter, and beamed at me good-naturedly, his face dissolving into a thousand wrinkles.

"Morning, Sir! Lovely morning too isn't it? Now what will you be having Sir?"

I leaned on the bar and looked closely at him.

"Surely it's Harry? You're Harry Fielding aren't you?"

He peered at me quizzically.

"That I am! Harry Fielding I've been for sixty five years, and hope to be for thirty more, if the good Lord be willing! But I'm that sorry Sir–I'm afraid I can't place you . . .?"

"Remember Tim Hunter?"

He stared at me incredulously, his bright blue eyes opening wide.

"By Heaven! You're never Tim Hunter!"

"By Heaven! I am! And if I've changed that much in fifteen years Harry . . ."

He charged through the flap in the counter, and was pumping my hand with such energy that I felt surely it must part company with my shoulder.

"Tim Hunter! My dear old Tim! Why fancy seeing you again lad! Many a time I thought you'd been killed in the War. Ah, no! You haven't changed, see? It's just that my memory for faces is that stupid and foggy, and I never seem to remember folks these days like when I was younger!"

Suddenly, he chuckled and propelled me to a table by the wall.

"Maybe my memory's not that bad after all, Tim me old lad! Watch this!"

He darted round the counter again, and returned with two brimming tankards.

"Drink that–and see if I can't remember what you always asked for! Cheers, boy!"

We drank deeply, and he wiped his mouth with the back of a great hand, and leaned across to me.

"Good?"

"Good! Don't worry about your memory Harry! You've taken me back twenty years with this! It's great!"

He roared with gusty laughter, then got up and eyed me appraisingly.

"You must be all of forty five, boy! You don't look it, by George! Are you married?"

I drained my tankard.

"Same again, Harry," I said. "Yes, I'm married. Two daughters."

"You've got your hands full then, I don't doubt!"

"Harry . . .?" I hesitated for a moment.

"Harry . . . do you remember a girl called Alison? . . ."

But it was too late! The door opened and two men, about my own age, walked in. Harry pounced on them.

"Come over here you two, and see who's turned up!"

For the next hour, in the confusion of handshakes and laughter and backslapping, I was unable to repeat my question.

Then, finally, the door closed behind the last customer. Harry was collecting the dirty glasses.

"There's a good home-made ham pie, and fresh salad in the back room. No, no, boy . . ."

He silenced my protest.

"It's already in there. The Missus won't be in until later on. She went to see her sister this morning."

Over Mrs Fielding's delicious pie, I was able to ask Harry my question about Alison again.

"Alison Moffat?" he said. "But she's Mrs Jim Clifford now you know."

"Yes, of course." I knew she married just after I left. "Does she still live here, Harry?"

Fascinated, I watched him cut into a ripe Stilton, and examine it with an expert eye.

"Up at the other end of the village, by Old Craddock's field, she lives now. Jim Clifford bought Garth House and a tidy bit of land there about six years ago. Good worker is Jim! Saves his money!"

He laid a piece of Stilton reverently on my plate.

"Took him a long time to get over the shock though."

"Shock?"

But at that moment the portly little form of Mrs Fielding entered the room and, afterwards, the conversation was monopolized by her eager, delighted questions.

It was nearly five o'clock when I drove along the road winding through the village, and skirted Old Craddock's field. Yes–there was the house! Low and white, with an air of sturdy elegance about its small Georgian door and green shuttered windows.

When I saw her, I knew why I had come! She was tall and lovely and carried herself with almost careless grace. Her hair was as smooth and black and shining as it had ever been. But her eyes had changed. They were still as blue as Canterbury bells–but there was no laughter. Only a strange, haunting sadness. Her hand flew to her mouth with a familiar gesture, and she gave a little cry.

"Tim! I can hardly believe it! Oh, Tim! I didn't recognize you at first . . ."

"It was the signpost," I said. "I was taking a short cut across the Mendips to the Midlands, and I saw the name of the village. I–I just felt I had to see how things had gone with you . . ."

Without any hesitation, she took my hand and led me into a long, pleasant lounge with a wonderful view of the hills and valleys.

"I don't have to ask if you are happy, Alison." I spoke with conviction.

This house bore the stamp of charm and beauty. It was the house of a woman who knew the happiness of a good marriage and had fulfilled her capacity for creating pleasure and comfort, by enriching every corner of her home. She smiled.

155

"It's so good to see you again, Tim! Yes, I've been very lucky. I have everything I need."

She handed me a cigarette box.

"Now, I'm sure you'd like some tea–but tell me first . . . How have things fared with you?"

I told her of my wife and daughters. I, too, had been fortunate in my marriage.

But all the time, I was longing to put the laughter back into her eyes.

When later I met Jim, I liked him instinctively–as indeed I had always liked him when we had been lads together. He was a huge, rosy-cheeked man who could have been shatteringly hearty, but who had instead a gentleness, sincerity and quiet strength. Their twelve year old daughter, Susan, burst in during tea. I smiled at her warmly and she responded instantly, with a clear, refreshing sparkle in her bright eyes. She helped herself to a scone from the tea trolley, stood vague and stork-like on one leg, then vanished from the room, leaving a thin "excuse me!" hanging like a vapour trail in her wake. We smiled knowingly at each other and I suddenly felt very much at home with these two charming, friendly people. We laughed and smoked and talked over old times, and the sun was fast disappearing over the hills as I rose to go.

"I'll come with you as far as the Common!" Alison said quickly. "I promised to go and see my mother. I'll just dash upstairs for a jacket."

Casually I glanced round the room, and noticed a lovely little oak bureau behind Jim's chair. I walked over and, as I stooped to examine it, I saw the small, framed photo of a young boy, almost hidden by a bowl of pink roses.

"Forgive me for being rude, Jim."

I turned and saw that he was standing now beside me.

"I never could resist a fine piece of furniture."

As I spoke, I felt a fierce compulsion to look again at the boy's face. I even turned the picture a little towards me, so that I could see it better. Jim's voice had a directness and simplicity that I found unnerving.

"Our son! He was run over and killed by a lorry at Bridgewater two years ago!"

There was nothing I could say. He had turned towards the hall–and as I gripped his hand and murmured goodbye–I knew I had never liked a man more.

Alison preceded me down the stone-flagged path, her hands in the pockets of her gay, yellow jacket. Fifteen years since I last saw her, I thought, and how lovely she is. She walks like a queen and strides like a gypsy. My poor, poor Alison. Now I know why the sadness is in your eyes.

Silently I drove until I reached the edge of the Common. Then I stopped the car and handed her a cigarette. As I lit it for her I said gently,

"I saw your son's photograph, and Jim told me what happened. I just want to say how sorry I am . . . He looked a fine lad. How old was he?"

"He would have been fourteen this year!" Her eyes filled with tears.

"I'm a fool to have mentioned it!" I said quickly." I'm sorry! I just felt I couldn't leave you without speaking about him . . ."

She raised her head, and gazed across the Common, as it slowly turned to gold in communion with the evening sky.

"He was yours Tim! Your son . . ."

It was peaceful up there on the Common. And quiet. I heard only the steady ticking of the clock on the dashboard, and the gentle breathing of the woman by my side.

I remembered another golden evening, such as this, when I was a young officer of thirty, home on leave. And Alison–sweet, generous Alison, had been a radiant twenty four.

It had been our last few hours together and I never saw her again. A year later, I had married a young nurse stationed with me overseas. Before my widowed mother left the village I heard that Alison had married Jim Clifford, and I had posted them a cheque for a wedding present. Now–I felt very, very humble. Alison stubbed out her cigarette without looking at me.

"Jim loved Paul as if he were his own son," she said slowly.

"Then he knew?" I asked. She nodded.

"I wouldn't have cheated him. He's a very fine man."

She put out her hand and I held it firmly in both of mine.

"You'll never come again," she said. It was a statement, not a question.

I looked at her steadily.

"I shall never come again, Alison. For your sake, and Jim's and Susan's. And thank you so very much for telling me about Paul."

I leaned forward, and kissed her gently on her smooth cheek. Her voice was sweet in my ear.

"I felt I had to tell you Tim. I wanted you to know."

I turned the car down to the village road and watched her tall figure stride towards her mother's house. She stood for a moment and waved to me, and as I drove away, I felt a throbbing, physical ache with the longing to comfort her.

The Days Of My Summer

On the edge of sleep, I sometimes think of Grandad's boxed-in lavatory, where I could drum my heels against the panelling and listen to the sweet talk of his caged pigeons. In the trembling heat of summer or when winter moons appeared in daytime skies I was sure of being undisturbed in that musty privacy.

Grandad lived in a grey street which merged into another grey street and went nowhere. Twice a week, after school, I called on him. I never minded listening to this old man with wrinkles stitched across his face, because he always gave me seed cake and a garden apple.

He would sit in his worn chair, staring at the blue above the chimney pots.

"Those were the lost mornings of my life, child. I was in the trenches at eighteen."

Because I knew his milky eyes would soon be turning in my direction, I always screwed up my face in concentration.

"A million lads fell out there in Flanders," he said. "Why did they have to die?"

I munched my seed cake, knowing he needed no answer. His papery hands would clench the arm of his chair.

"Because they had no choice, child. They obeyed orders. They were murdered."

Before I left him, I usually visited the garden hut which he still insisted on keeping, even though by then he had an indoor bathroom. The wooden throne had a warm and sensual contact with my skin. Above the rickety shelf piled with disused flowerpots I could see the glassed square of sky almost blocked by straggling roses. Feeling safe and mysterious, I would fractionally open the door to admit the neighbouring tabby to rub his soft flat face against my legs, filling my kingdom with his friendly purrs. Sitting there in the stillness, I would think of blue summers and long grass, with my mother's hair, dark as ink, seeming polished in the sunlight of our picnic years. Sprawled in the meadow, young and strong, my father had been untroubled by responsibility, while at his feet my baby brother pulled buttercups with fat, indiscriminate fingers, his rounded chin downy with pollen.

In the seclusion of the shed I would fondle the cat's velvet ears as it weaved around me. I knew that things were changing and the days of my summer were over, but I was too young to know what 'strike' and 'depression' meant and why 'blackleg' was shouted at my father.

I would leave Grandad and hurry home along the deserted streets, past the beehive sounds of anger from the meeting hall, past the silent shops accusingly shuttered.

Young as I was, I sensed that the quietness of my small town had become a sinister and brooding presence.

Where I belong

Morning short story
Friday 18th October 1963

The manager was eyeing me doubtfully.

"You know this lady Sir?"

I glanced at the tall, dark-haired girl standing by the desk, with the stocky figure of the store detective beside her still holding the gloves she had been accused of stealing.

"I know the lady very well," I said coldly. "I can assure you a dreadful mistake has been made. I asked her to buy these gloves and put them on my account, and it was obvious she was holding them in her hand while she looked around for one or two other things . . ."

The manager glanced at the detective, who stared impassively in front of him. I knew that neither of them believed me, but I was relying on their knowledge of me as a City businessman and a very good account customer. The manager turned towards me again.

"Mr Perkins could have been mistaken of course . . ."

I saw the cold eyes of the detective flicker with distaste, and I felt momentarily sick at my deceit, but I merely glanced coolly at my wristwatch.

"Naturally he was mistaken. I can only consider it fortunate that this lady mentioned my name and that you had the courtesy to get in touch with me. Otherwise I should not have hesitated to carry this entire matter to your Directors!"

The bluff worked and the manager rose hastily.

"That won't be necessary of course, Mr Reeves. We have your word, and I apologise for any distress caused to either of you."

He bowed to Helen who had not uttered a sound during the whole interview. Gently, I took her arm, knowing from my experience of other occasions that she was completely dazed, and praying they had not smelled the whisky on her breath. She was hatless and wore an old belted raincoat. But she was so beautiful, even then, with her dark blue eyes and raven hair, that people turned to watch us as I led her from the store. Thankful that my office block was just around the corner, I guided her to my car, and she sank wearily into the back seat. For a moment, a flicker of recognition came into her eyes, and her long fingers caressed the upholstery.

"Nice!" she said sleepily. "Nice and comfy!"

And that was all. I leaned over her, and tucked the rug around her with practised hands, cursing myself for having listened to her pleas to drive her into the City on my way to work that morning. But then, I always did listen. I loved her very much, and you cannot resist for long the entreaties of someone you love–even though you know you cannot trust them. Her eyes were closed now and she looked suddenly dignified and yet so very vulnerable, with her mouth drooping at the corners and her dark, silky hair falling across her forehead. I pushed it gently away, knowing I should be angry with her but feeling only the fierce tenderness and compassion that bound me to her as surely as it had ever done.

It had always been the same . . . She had become a vital part of my life when I was nineteen and so unsure of my emotions that my façade of being a man of the world deceived no one. Helen least of all. Her parents had died when she was four years old and she lived with her aunt who ran a thriving little dressmaking business in our country town. But I did not fall in love with her until I returned from College, and found a tall and lovely woman in place of the girl who had still been at school when I went away. I remember how I envied Helen her self assurance and the determination which made her so convinced the countryside was God forsaken and depressing.

"I don't know how you stand the place, Harry. It's so deadly! There's nothing to do here. Nothing I want to do, anyway!"

She made me feel even more restless and uncertain than I was already, because I knew I could never agree with her. I loved the country as passionately as she hated it, and I almost despised her at times for her intolerance. But I adored her too, for her vitality and the sheen of her long, black hair and the sparkle in her blue eyes.

Even now, as I drive her home in the late winter sunshine, the hills overlooking our little sleepy town are as vital to me as they have always been; the sighing and the rustling and the murmuring. I remember how I would lie there with my face cushioned against the moss and the heather, listening to the gentle stirrings beneath me, and breathing the richness and the peatiness of high summer. I could smell the sea in the west wind while the larks spiraled upwards, their bursting throats full of gladness and liquid song. And I had known then only the unhappiness of loving, and not being loved in return. My father had not been as understanding as I felt he should.

"I don't like to see you like this, boy!" he said gloomily. "You're worse than a lovesick calf!"

My answer must have sounded wretchedly dramatic, but I think he guessed I was sincere.

"I need her, Father, and I can't live without her. I love her."

He had looked at me in despair because he didn't know how to help me and my mother expected me to marry Dinah Reslaw, the pretty daughter of an old school friend. Dinah and I had known each other since childhood and, though I was very fond of her, I knew–and father knew–there was no excitement and no magic. Only a sameness of interests and a common belief of what was expected of us. How I hated the prospect! A good, safe marriage and growing old together in respectable and loveless harmony! I had thought my father didn't understand me, so help me. But I know now that he did, because he gave me the best advice he could think of, and if I'd taken it, I would have led at least, a placid and normal life.

"Marry Dinah, my boy! She'll make you happy enough, and you want to grasp all the happiness you can in this life. There's always shadow with ecstasy, lad! Stop reaching for the moon!"

Perhaps it was the June Ball that was the turning point. Helen had never looked more beautiful. Her aunt had made her a dress of rustling silk; a clear corn gold, which made her hair blacker than before, and her skin as white as milk. The great barn was transformed into a fairyland of orange, red and yellow Chinese lanterns, with tubs of snowy marguerites and bonfires of marigolds simmering in dark corners. It was a warm and splendid night, and I only wish I could look back on it with gaiety and laughter, for it was a setting worthy of it. But I can only remember the twisting hatred I felt for Jack Sanderson, because he had brought to Helen's lovely face a radiance and warmth that I had never–in all my loving of her–been able to do. He had been working in the town for two months and, in my folly, I had ignored him as indeed I would have ignored anyone as being a possible rival for my beloved Helen. Looking back now, I can laugh at my youthful conceit, but it wasn't funny then.

I remember standing in a corner, holding the dish of strawberry ice-cream that Helen had asked me to bring her, and staring emptily at her laughing face lifted towards Jack as he bent over her chair talking softly to her. I didn't hear what he was saying. I only remember, as I moved towards them, the expression in her eyes and the gentleness of her mouth and my own awareness of absolute defeat as she took the ice-cream from my outstretched hand. She smiled up at me, her eyes radiant.

"Harry, you've met Jack, haven't you? He's the new representative for Lockwood's Pickles."

He nodded at me. He was very confident and I disliked the small neatness of his head and the arrogant way it was set on the large, muscular body. But I couldn't deny the overpowering and compelling attraction of his voice and personality.

"Hallo, Harry. Grand night for dancing, eh? And incidentally it's chutney old lad, not pickle!"

He turned to smile down at Helen and I wanted to crush my fingers into his neck, as with a small, intimate movement, his hand brushed her cheek.

"Chutney sounds better now, doesn't it?" The hand slid caressingly to her shoulder. "Will you dance with me, lady in the yellow dress?"

The way she handed me the ice-cream dish was almost a gesture of dismissal and I watched despairingly as they melted into the crowd, helpless and alone in my knowledge of having lost her.

In the weeks which followed, of course, it was a fruitless battle all the way. The fight goes out of you when you don't stand a chance of winning the prize. I met her for the last time as she was striding across the meadows to her aunt's house through tall grasses, lacquered gold by the evening sun. She always had a wonderful way of walking, with a poise that had a spun glass beauty, and a rhythm that was the integral and vital expression of her whole personality. As I approached her she held out her hand to me, but I saw again that same quiet pity creep into her eyes, and I knew suddenly–as surely as I knew anything–that I must not plead with her, or tell her how much I loved her. Instead, I caught her hand in mine, and drew her into my arms. Quietly I held her there for a moment, then I kissed her and walked quickly away.

The Secret

Morning Story
26th August 1965

She looked at herself in the mirror, and saw lines of weariness and resignation forming already on her face.

Twenty years ago, her warm, brown eyes had sparkled like sunlight on water and her mouth had curved upwards in joy. Now her world had lost its spring-bright promise and disillusion had become her shield.

She could never quite pinpoint the moment when Tom had ceased to love her. Perhaps it was because she was childless, and yet she had always hoped that their marriage would succeed in spite of this, drawing them together in mutual understanding.

From upstairs came the early morning movements which meant that Tom would soon be ready for his breakfast. Slowly, she put bacon in a pan and prepared a pot of coffee with an indifference which had long ago replaced her pride in household tasks.

Her husband clumped downstairs and stood yawning hugely and running his great hands through hair crisp as coir matting. Without a word she placed his breakfast on the table, and poured coffee for them both. There was something about this morning that she couldn't understand. A kind of suppressed excitement, so different from his usual blank, disinterested stare.

"Anything wrong, Tom?"

She sipped her coffee, and looked at him over the rim of her cup.

He shrugged his shoulders, deliberately subduing his mood. He always underplayed his emotions to her. Never revealing. Never relaxing.

"There's something on your mind" she persisted.

Slowly he said, "Well, yes there is, but I want to make sure of one or two details first. It can wait until later for me to tell you."

Excited, because even so small an admission was unusual for him, she asked him again.

"What is it then? Why can't you tell me just a little?"

He rose hastily.

"There's a lot of orders to get off today," he said. "I shall probably be home pretty late. Ten o'clock maybe."

She looked across at him, knowing how he mistrusted her, and hating his secrecy. Her mind had been hazy with memories ever since she had woken that morning and had realised their twentieth anniversary was the very next day. Twenty years tomorrow! Years of joy and famine. Better, she thought miserably, that a marriage should be murdered violently and passionately than it should die from malnutrition as theirs had surely done. He had walked across to the door and she noticed, suddenly, the expression on his face, half impatient, half reticent.

Grudgingly, he said, "I'll let you know tomorrow. You'll be pleased about it. It will be a surprise."

Then, as though he had said too much, he reached quickly for his jacket and she heard his footsteps crunching down the garden path. She watched him from the window as he opened the garage doors and backed the estate car into the driveway.

He was self assured and competent in all his actions, and she knew he expected others to be the same. That was why she disappointed him. She was too emotional, too intense. Her desires were not his desires and she found him cold and clinical, where her own natural reactions were warm and responsive.

She returned to the breakfast table and sat frowning into her cup, his words flooding into her mind. It simply wasn't like Tom to get excited and yet he had certainly been agitated over something this morning. A surprise, he'd said, and tomorrow was their anniversary. Surely it couldn't be that! And yet, after all, the twentieth year was a milestone, and even Tom might have paused from his idolatry of his market garden to look back, as she did, recalling the good times as well as the bad.

They hadn't been out together for years because of the constant flow of orders for flowers and vegetables from his beloved nurseries. She remembered how frequently he had come home with tickets for a theatre or a dance before he had become totally immersed in the business. Perhaps it was not too late to forget the empty years. Maybe Tom had already resolved that tomorrow was as good a day as any to do just that.

Her excitement high, she rose from the table, overwhelmingly certain that his secrecy could only mean that he was taking her somewhere as an anniversary surprise. All female, suddenly, she wondered desperately what she would wear. Her wardrobe consisted of clothes to suit her working life, and if she wanted a dress for their anniversary, she would have to buy one today. She had saved a small amount of money from two weeks strawberry picking on a neighbouring farm, and now she counted the notes and prayed it would be enough to buy her something new. Something that would make Tom proud of her and revive his interest in her.

She performed her household tasks that morning with a joy she had not known for years. Tom would be busy all day delivering orders for a large wedding being held in the next town and, she decided with all-consuming happiness, to purchase the new dress that afternoon.

She often remembered afterwards how beauty was etched on her mind that day as she cycled into town. The richness of blues and greens; the shimmer of poplars; a frenzy of late roses on the cottage walls. Over everything there lay a stillness and peace to mark the ending of a golden summer. The dress was perfect, in pleated silk, as yellow as a cornfield to complement her once-bright hair. She bore her parcel home, a symbol of triumph, and spent the next few hours finding pleasure in housework, where apathy had always been. Later, in the seclusion of her bedroom she twirled before the mirror in delight, revelling in her longings and hopes, and renewing her belief that she and Tom could recapture their lost joy.

When he came home that evening, very late, she had prepared his favourite meal. He seemed mellow and happy as after supper he filled his pipe.

"Don't bother about the dishes, Lucy. Sit outside for a while. It's a warm night on the terrace."

Slowly, she followed him, sensing again his hidden excitement, and trying desperately to keep her own emotions under control.

There was a strange expression on his face as he looked out at the garden, black and silver in the summer night. He discarded his pipe and turned towards her, and for the first time he didn't stare away and beyond her, but talked to her with meaning and warmth in his voice as he had in their earlier years.

"Tomorrow," he said. "It's a big day . . . "

He paused and looked at her curiously, and she realised she must be staring at him with almost fearful longing. A small frown appeared between his eyes as he continued.

"Tomorrow is going to affect both of us. It means a great deal . . . "

Again he broke off, and she was unable to curb her eagerness.

"Yes, Tom? Tomorrow. What is it?"

His mood of elation was gone, and with it his desire to impart his secret.

"Never mind. It will keep."

She made a tremendous effort. She mustn't press him or he might cancel all his plans. Instead she shrugged her shoulders nonchalantly.

"Of course. Let it keep. I'll wash up now, Tom. It's getting late."

All the time she prepared for bed, her pleasure mounted. She felt that tomorrow was a turning point, but she couldn't analyse her feelings. She knew only a simple joy in the belief that she and Tom could find—if not an ecstasy—at least a comfort in their marriage, and a giving, one to the other. She heard his slow, unhurried movements, the ritual of door-locking and pipe-tapping, and then his heavy tread on the stairs. He undressed as he had always done in the twenty years of their life together; ponderously, with a careful folding of clothes and a sense of purpose in all his actions. Usually, she turned away from him when she felt his heaviness beside her, but tonight she lay on her back, her eyes bright and warm. He glanced at her in surprise, as though sensing the change in her, then he, too, seemed to relax a little.

"Not tired, Lucy?"

Her response was immediate. Perhaps this twentieth milestone in their lives would bring a new understanding and awareness. Tomorrow would surely be a day to remember, and Tom had decided, as well as she, to restore all they had lost.

Warmth flooded her again as through an open window came the midnight chimes of the church clock. She turned towards him impulsively.

"Yes."

He was elated. "Tomorrow will be my final payment on the business after all these years. It's ours from tomorrow, Lucy. Or today if you like! The land, the greenhouses. Everything!"

The hand that lay in the crook of his arm went suddenly limp, but he failed to observe it. His voice was animated, almost emotional.

"I went to the Bank today, and confirmed all the final arrangements. They're going to give me a big loan so I can expand even further."

He looked down at her, lying beside him.

"I've a feeling you probably guessed what I was so pleased about this morning, Lucy, but I couldn't tell you until I'd been to the Bank, and had everything transferred to me. You know how I always like to be certain of my facts."

Peevishly, he noticed at last, that she wasn't sharing his joy. That was just like Lucy! She attached so much importance to the little things, and never appreciated the events in her life which really mattered. He decided to give her another chance, and he leaned across her, clumsy in his movements.

"Come on, old girl. This really is something to celebrate. It's a big day on the calendar for us!!! Tell you what, if I develop a new strain of rose, I'll call it after you. How about that, now? Would 'Madame Lucy' suit you? Can you think of anything better?"

Blindly, she reached up and shut off the light, hating his magnanimous mood, and knowing he would not understand the naked disappointment in her face. All the hungering in twenty years for a delicacy of love which had never been hers was reflected now in the bitterness of her voice.

Wearily, she said,

"A new rose? Perhaps you could call it 'Anniversary'!" and turned hopelessly away from his puzzled face towards the familiar wall . . .

Procter, Procter

The first chapter of a children's book.

"You must be mistaken," said her mother. "Why ever should Miss Procter be staying at this hotel?"

"How should I know? Perhaps she likes Scotland." Sarah's fear made her speak crossly.

"Anyway, I definitely saw her signing the register an hour ago."

She pushed away her plateful of food because she wasn't very hungry But she WAS very frightened. Her father frowned and tapped his teeth, which meant that he was trying to remember something.

"Miss Procter always reminded me of a predatory currant bun, with stick arms and legs," he said. "I wonder if she's still teaching?"

"What's predatory?" asked Tom.

"Waiting and watching," said Sarah, with the authority of being three years older than her brother.

"Usually with a view to eating people," grinned Mr Hayward.

Tom wasn't listening.

"She was a horrible teacher. I hated her. She was short and fat and grumpy."

'She was also strange,' thought Sarah. 'Very strange indeed.'

She tried to recall that end-of-term morning several years ago at the local school, when the classroom of children had been at their noisiest, with Sarah herself as their ringleader, singing 'Procter, Procter, call the Doctor. If he'll come, she'll cane his bum!'

The headmistress had swept in from the corridor, furious at seeing an unattended class and angrily clapping her hands.

When, minutes later, Miss Procter arrived, the headmistress had reprimanded her in front of her pupils, and Sarah had shuddered and looked away as she saw the hostility in the small, unblinking eyes of their teacher. And in the smile that turned into a sneer.

Soon afterwards, when they'd broken up for the summer, something horrible had happened, which Sarah had deliberately erased from her mind, because she was looking forward to senior school in September . . .

"She's probably with a coach-party," her mother was saying as she rose from the table. "I expect they'll only stay for a couple of nights."

As they left the dining-room, a husky voice made them turn towards a dumpy figure, dressed in a red blouse and a long, black skirt.

"It's Sarah and Tom Maynard, isn't it?" Miss Procter said. "Fancy meeting you here." She was staring at Sarah. "Let me see, you must be about fifteen. My, how tall you are, dear."

Sarah's mother, who had never liked her children's form mistress, put on the polite face which she reserved for solicitors and bank managers.

"Are you staying for long, Miss Procter?"

The schoolmistress beamed at her.

"Just the week."

Sarah wanted to get right away from this woman who smiled only with her mouth. She clenched her hands and concentrated on their next day's plans to walk to the ferry boat which would take them to the island. Miss Procter looked at her and nodded.

"Ah, yes," she murmured. "I hear that's a delightful trip. The island is a bird sanctuary, you know."

She patted her crimped, grey hair as she turned to leave. "Anyway, we're sure to meet again, dears. Have fun."

Sarah glanced across at her parents. Her father didn't appear to have noticed anything unusual, but her mother seemed vaguely puzzled. For a moment, she shook her head as if to clear it, before she went upstairs, while Sarah suddenly shivered as her memories began to make a pattern.

The next morning, at breakfast, Miss Procter approached their table. Mr Hayward was courteous.

"It's a beautiful day. Will you be swimming in the pool, Miss Procter?"

"I think not," she said. "I prefer long walks."

Uneasily, Sarah noted the thick walking stick in the fat little hand and the stout, laced shoes. Surely Miss Procter wasn't also going to the island?

"Yes, perhaps I'll do that, dear. How very nice."

Sarah's father raised his eyebrows.

"Perhaps you'll do what, Miss Procter?"

"Come with you. On your walk to the ferry."

Sarah's heartbeats quickened.

"But we didn't ask you!"

Mrs Hayward, who would generally not have tolerated such rudeness, spoke very quickly.

"I'm sorry, Miss Procter, but we never really know what we're doing from day to day. We have no set plans."

"Well, naturally, I don't want to intrude on your family activities . . . "

As the stone-cold eyes fastened on her mother's face, all the pictures which Sarah had blotted out came pouring back, and she vividly recalled her fear and shock at the headlines in her local newspaper, a week or so after the noisy classroom incident. The lettering had been huge and black, dominating the page. 'HEADMISTRESS DROWNED IN THE THAMES IN SCHOOL HOLIDAYS.'

Once they were all outside in the cloudless morning, Sarah felt better. The hills were blue and misted. The climbing sun was almost overhead. They began the five-mile walk to the ferry, their feet disturbing the nesting larks as they followed the sheep-track through the heather. Something made Sarah look back while she could still see the hotel. Miss Procter was on the front steps, watching them, her motionless body seeming dark and angular. Determinedly, Sarah turned her face to the soft wind.

"Come on," she cried to Tom. "I'll race you to the Tor."

He was petulant. "You always win."

Mr Hayward chuckled.

"Never mind. She may be the best runner in her school, but you're the best cricketer in yours."

He smiled at Sarah as he spoke. She knew he was very proud that she had won so many cups and medals for her sprinting. He threw an arm around her shoulders.

"By the way, your mother and I are agreed that you're absolutely right about Miss Procter. We're beginning to intensely dislike that lady!"

They were two miles from the ferry, when they stopped and looked upwards, their faces distorted in terror. Before they could turn or speak they were overtaken by a black, spinning column, a giant water-spout between earth and sky, which tossed them around like puppets, lashing them with silver needles.

"Run!" shouted Mr Hayward, but wherever they went, the column held them.

They heard laughter as wild as a scream. Yet, from their fearful prison they could see the sun shining on the heather. The fragile harebells were untouched! With dramatic suddenness, the laughter ceased and the water-spout fell away from them as if suctioned by vacuum. They sprawled, exhausted, until, one by one, they struggled to their feet. When they reached their hotel, limping and bruised from their ordeal, Miss Procter was reading in the sun-lounge.

"My!" she said. "Aren't you in a state! Was there a storm somewhere?"

They stopped in front of her, their hair plastered in their faces. Several people sitting nearby wrinkled their noses at the odour of wet wool.

"What a stupid thing to ask!" Sarah had never heard such sharpness in her father's voice.

Miss Procter swung her head towards him with a snake-like movement and, as Sarah saw the unwinking eyes, she shuddered uncontrollably, reaching for the comfort of her mother's hand.

When they came down to dinner, Miss Procter was seated at her table, her little high-heeled shoes gripping the top rung of her chair, because her legs weren't long enough to reach the floor. As they walked past her to cross the long dining-hall, she said,

"Are you coming on the coach trip to Fort William tomorrow?"

Abruptly they turned. Mr Hayward spoke harshly.

"No, we are not."

Sarah hugged to herself the knowledge that they had all made a decision to drive to the HIghlands for the next few days. She was conscious that Miss Procter had been staring at her, although she was now studying her painted nails.

"That's a lovely idea," she said. "I've always adored the HIghlands. I'd be happy to share in the petrol with you."

Sarah was frightened by the bewilderment in her father's eyes, but his voice was firm and cold.

"We're going alone," he said. "Just as a family. I thought we'd made that clear."

Miss Procter merely hummed and rubbed a finger round the rim of her wine glass, as she watched them walk away from her.

As the meal progressed, Mr Hayward grew quieter, pushing his food in small heaps on his plate, his head lowered. Soon after the main course, he rose without a word, his body stiff, his legs moving like a guardsman as he strode between the tables, unheeding his wife as she called to him. Faster and faster he ran, gathering incredible speed as he approached the glass doors, which had been left open in the hot, August night. As her mother screamed, Sarah pushed aside her chair. She launched herself with practised rhythm, her long legs thrusting her forward.

Her father was already in the garden, heading for the river which surged beyond the hotel grounds towards a downstream weir. She could see his face, now, as she drew level. His eyes were wide and sightless and his breath came in painful gasps. She gained on him as they reached the swirling water, throwing herself sharply in front of him and wincing when his foot crashed into her ribs. He stumbled to the soft turf, sitting up almost immediately, blinking and rubbing his head.

Sarah rose, holding her side, as her mother and Tom raced towards her. Behind them, she saw something they didn't.

High over an apple tree a rotund figure floated, balloon-like, twirling and dipping in the dying light, bouncing and bobbing until it mingled with a trail of stars.

As Sarah put her arm around Tom's shoulders, she heard a shrill, triumphant cackle from the silver sky, and with a blinding awareness of the power of both love and evil, she knew with certainty that Miss Procter would return.

A Woman's Impressions Of China

1987

We were bent almost double in the chanting procession of Chinese six-year olds, as we pranced conga-fashion around the schoolroom in our version of 'Chase the Dragon'.

These children of China are entrancing with their doll-like faces and black shining hair. Half an hour before, their eyes, dark as chestnuts, had widened in polite amazement as we edged apologetically into their kindergarten. The young teacher with the golden skin and full sweet mouth had bowed her head in welcome as she played the prim harmonium, which surely once belonged in the pioneering mission-halls.

Guilin kindergarten 1987

179

In one corner of the stone flagged room, a charcoal stove showed a brave square of crimson. In Soochow that day it was cold enough for the snow that we had left eight hundred miles north in Peking. We had expected warmth in this area, renowned for its silk and the beauty of its women, but the Spring clung grimly still to Winter. The windows were open to the Siberian winds, and we realised why the children, butterfly-bright in their oranges and purples, wore several layers of sweaters and jackets with their padded trousers. There was no heating anywhere, apart from that defiant little stove!

With the exception of our splendid hotels, we found this bone-chilling cold and mania for fresh air in every public building in China, be it museum, shop or factory, until we finally reached the spring-like temperatures of Canton. Young and old, they were impervious to the rawness outside. No arms slapping across chests; no blowing on frozen fingers. We from the West, denied even the temporary comfort of a heated lunchtime restaurant, grew bleaker as the days went by. They watched us with expressions both kindly and curious.

There were as yet so few tourists in this land of bicycles and paddy fields that we were surrounded wherever we went by friendly people in their unisex trousers and tunics, even in the larger towns. Not once in those pleasant faces did we see envy.

"There is no need for us to envy you," explained Su-Li, our young and pretty interpreter, drawing her straight black brows together in an effort to convince us. "We have no property and everyone is equal. All are housed in high-rise apartment or street or river dwelling. Rental for these is five per cent of salary. No one is jobless. The State provides."

She paused for a moment before she gently added, "and crime is almost unknown."

Her fine-boned face was serene, her every action as delicate as the ringed cormorants on the bamboo fishing rafts. Here was a student of China, intelligent, versatile and witty, in a land where women now hold equality with men.

That morning at breakfast she had declared, "I shall not marry until I am twenty five."

"Why not?' we asked her. "Suppose you married before that age?"

"I would be allowed only three days honeymoon," she said. "If I wait until the State suggests, I will be granted fifteen days."

"And only one child per family?" we persisted.

She nodded, unperturbed.

"Our fathers had too many sons. Now the old have pensions and their children do not have to support them. It is a wise law."

Curious, we asked, "Do you mind?"

"Not in the least," she replied. "Our child will be loved and cherished."

"What is the penalty for having more than one?" asked a lady who had four children back in England.

"We lose all our State allowances," said Su-Li. She was smiling.

An American tourist passing our table said, "Guess that means plenty of abortions, huh?"

Still smiling Su-Li gave an almost imperceptible shrug.

Apart from their forward planning for a selective generation, this is a land of long-ago, where the bicycle and handcart dominate the streets and the abacus is still forerunner to the tills in the computerless stores. As our coach hooted its way through swarms of incredibly competent cyclists, there was a snapshot in every moment of the crowded day. Old men play chequers on a pavement table, their wrinkled faces tranquil and absorbed beneath their flat, peaked caps. Women hang washing on lines which stretch relentlessly from tree to tree along the very edge of the main streets. They stop to lift their solitary offspring high on their shoulders, as we applaud yet another exquisite baby. An old woman sits on the kerb, preparing vegetables in an enamel basin. Before her unseeing eyes, the passing crowd could be a poem or a painting. The slim young men of China, in their tight-tight denims and mass-produced shirts barely glance at the small straight girls, some with features so delightful that words like porcelain and lotus flower form easily in the mind.

The endless stream of handcarts are a way of life. A houseful of furniture and perhaps a high-perched infant and a crate of chickens on their moving day. Eggs and cabbages and ducks for market. Bamboo poles for scaffolding. Coal, meat and fish. And junk that would fill a thousand western scrapyards!

Later that day, a heavy rainstorm took us by surprise. There was a light touch on my arm.

"Please allow me?"

A pretty girl with waist length hair tied back from her face in an ebony knot, linked my arm under her pink umbrella.

"I learn English at night school," she explained. "This is my father."

She indicated a bespectacled, middle-aged man in collarless jacket and the eternal peaked cap.

"He is university professor."

He bowed, appearing so happy to meet us that we were suddenly humbled. We found this same friendliness wherever we travelled in that gentle land.

China, while indescribably rich in culture, is poor in modern facilities, apart from their superb and luxurious tourist hotels. Public toilets in restaurants, for instance, were generally appalling. The American women tourists accustomed, perhaps even more than Europeans, to super-hygiene, would emerge from the cubicles with scarves and handkerchiefs over nose and mouth.

"Oh my God!" they would scream. "If you're goin' in there honey, slide in BACKWARDS for pity's sake. That way, you don't figure to SEE them!"

Most of us prefer the 'hole-in-the-ground' type. At least everything had discreetly vanished! The Americans valiantly tried, but simply couldn't master them.

"Goddam it, Mary Lou," moaned one to her companion. "Ah've peed all over my trousers!"

Nevertheless, they were generous in offering us protective toilet-seat covers, which they had with them in large plastic bags. My friend and I politely refused, as we had never even contemplated getting near enough those seats to actually SIT on them, having already perfected an aim worthy of a wartime bomber.

Back to the swarming streets. Dodge those pedal—pushers. Love those children, standing to stare at us, their legs sturdily apart, while their multi-layers of bright clothing made their arms stick out like walking toys. Life-sized, lovable dolls with their laughing faces and inquisitive eyes.

Until recently, spitting had been a national pastime. Although it is now banned, many of the older generation cannot rid themselves of this lifetime habit. We learned to be wary! My friend, who was walking beside my husband, heard him clearing his throat. Without a moment's hesitation, she leaped to one side. Perhaps that's why they have so many zig-zag paths!

Although the Forbidden City and the Great Wall and the Terracotta Army stunned and overawed me, my unexpected moment of pure emotion came towards the end of our stay. We were driving back to our hotel, still enchanted by our boat trip on the sapphire rivers which meander through the serrated mountains of Guilin.

"I will sing you a song of farewell," said our guide.

Her reed-thin, lilting voice set an old, old story to a near Celtic melody. Maybe it was a tourist performance, but as we watched her quiet face on that fragile evening, we preferred to think it was spontaneous.

I looked out across the flat landscape where the water buffaloes, awaiting their wooden plough, stood patient in the paddy fields. Families were planting rice in small emerald bunches in their allotted squares of dark water. The sun's horizontal rays burnished the distant hills.

Just over that border, I saw in my mind's eye, the sky-scrapers of Hong Kong and the razzamatazz and high technology that we call civilisation. Another story, I thought. Another world.

Fleetingly saddened, I turned away from my window, as on the faintest whisper the guide ended her sweet song.

Homecoming

Three and a half years on, the telegram said 'Meet me at Portsmouth Central—midnight. Longing to see you.'

I duly took a taxi (no private cars in 1946) and walked across the station concourse which was depressingly lit by four naked bulbs. Some bored military policemen leaned against the closed shutters of the bookstall and a sailor seated on a wooden bench was being violently sick.

For the homecoming, I had always visualised a country cottage (don't ask me why) and a garden path leading to a wooden gate. I had recently seen Laurence Olivier in Wuthering Heights and I rather fancied a Heathcliff! Heathcliff! situation, in slow motion, with outstretched arms as my husband opened the garden gate and ran towards me.

The sailor was being sick again and I turned to concentrate on the train now trundling into the station.

He was the only one who alighted and we peered from either end of the platform and began to walk towards each other. (Heathcliff! Heathcliff! Where were the outstretched arms; my flying hair; the long, drifting strides?)

He bent to kiss me. Wildly, I thought, 'I don't remember a moustache! Surely he didn't have it when he went away?'

For a long moment, after years of aching separation and hundreds of 'When we meet again' letters, we stared at each other in silence.

Then, "How are you?" he asked . . .

I looked up at this tall stranger. I spoke almost primly—I even shook his hand.

"I'm very well, thank you!!!" I said.

With Joan's dog 1943

On Southsea beach 1939

Phillip's photo

Epcot Centre 1989

The Coach House 2004

Lightning Source UK Ltd.
Milton Keynes UK
UKOW052354071111

181630UK00002B/26/P